SCOTTY

and the

LOST DUTCHMAN MINE

by

BETTY SWINFORD

MOODY PRESS

CHICAGO

Printed in the United States of America

CONTENTS

1

FIRST NIGHT OUT

THERE WAS KEEN EXCITEMENT in Scotty Hanson's brown eyes. "I mean it, Danny, you've never seen anything like this place!"

Danny looked at his friend without smiling. "You've said that a hundred times! Now cut it out, will you, until I've had a chance to see for myself?"

Scotty caught his father's glance in the rear view mirror. They both grinned. *They* knew! If no one else in the whole world knew, they did.

They'd been hunting in the Superstition Mountains last fall, when they'd found it. Or rather, stumbled into it! And all their vivid descriptions and accounts had failed to arouse much interest in the rest of the family. Probably because they thought Scotty and his dad were exaggerating. Well, they'd see in a couple of minutes now that this tiny paradise valley really did exist!

The jeep clambered on, over the rocks that covered what was once a narrow trail. Catclaw and ocotillo reached out to scrape the sides of the jeep. Like they were trying to hold them back. And jumping cactus caused both Danny and Scotty to duck quickly back inside the safety of the jeep.

It was Susan, Scotty's sister, who showed no enthusiasm. None! Of course, she *was* the only girl on the trip. Her friend Mary had had to cancel out and go to California with her parents after all.

Danny suddenly hunched down in his seat to peer up through the window at something. "Hey! Isn't that the famous Weaver's Needle?"

Scotty sucked in his breath. "Sure is! One of the landmarks of the Lost Dutchman Gold Mine! That's it, all right."

Danny half turned in his seat, which wasn't easy because of all the camping gear packed around him. "Tell me about the mine, Scot. Everything you know about it."

Scotty gave his friend a twisted smile and stuck his nose in the air. "I've told you dozens of times already."

"Come on, Scotty!" Danny's blue eyes mirrored the usual twinkle. "I can't even remember the old prospector's last name."

Susan squirmed miserably. "I don't even know his *first* name, and *I* don't care!"

Mrs. Hanson suddenly gasped. The jeep had just risen over a steep hill and was moving cautiously upward along the ridge.

"Mother, what's wrong?" Susan forgot her own dismal thoughts and sat forward. "Why—what is it?"

Mr. Hanson stopped the vehicle on the crest of the hill, his brown hands tight against the steering wheel. "This is our valley, honey." He looked more than just pleased. "Disappointed?"

His wife was breathing rapidly. "Oh, it's beautiful! I never dreamed there could be a place like this in the Superstition Mountains!"

Susan was oh-ing and ah-ing. "And a waterfall coming right out of those rocks to form that pool! I can't believe it! It's dreamy!"

Danny stared, eyes wide and mouth ajar. "Cool!" he breathed. "Real cool!"

Scotty emerged from the jeep and stood on the crest of the hill. He and his dad had hardly believed their eyes the first time. Now, seeing it again, it still didn't seem possible that cradled in this maze of dry hills and cactus there could be a spot like this.

Susan and Danny got out of the jeep too, and Mr. Hanson drove slowly down into the tiny valley.

Catclaw reached out for the three youths, snatching their jeans. Rabbit brush was everywhere. It looked like everything was brown; while before their eyes was a tiny valley so lovely it seemed like a dream. Lush green grass. Wild flowers. Great cottonwood trees instead of desert mesquite and palo verde. A long, golden sandbar. And the water that made it all possible. Rushing from rocks five feet above, at the mouth of this little valley, water tumbled and splashed like diamonds. Then, dropping down to the valley floor, it laughed and giggled on, forming its own bed, to disappear again later at the end of the valley, and so return once more to the underground stream.

"One of Mother Nature's tricks," Susan murmured. "Wonderful! Letting that water go free just long enough to bring something so beautiful out of something so brown and ugly."

Scotty watched his sister. Wasn't that just like her, all dignified and poised and talking her head off like a poet! He had to admit, though, that he would have been terribly disappointed if she had not liked his valley.

"And we only have five days here," Danny moaned.

Susan began bouncing down the hill toward the valley. "Well, I'm not going to waste a single minute!" she declared.

Scotty pushed back the shock of unruly brown hair that fell over his forehead—only to have it fall again a moment later. He left it there. He missed Butch, his bulldog. But—just in case there was *someone* here who had made all the past accidents happen, they didn't want to chance the dog's barking.

Susan had pulled off her tennis shoes and was walking up and down the stretch of warm sand. The look of wonder on her face said that maybe she would have a good time after all. And she certainly *was* glad she'd brought her bathing suit.

"Who would ever believe this?" Mrs. Hanson was drinking in the beauty and breathing deeply of the clear mountain air.

Scotty took the skillet out of her hand and placed it on the grill that he and his father had left there from their past hunting trip. From there, he called back to his mother, "Tonight I'll take you back to the hill, Mom. You can see back the way we came for miles and miles. It's like looking into another world."

Danny ran up breathlessly. "Did you know there's a natural bathtub to one side of that waterfall? It's an oblong basin made of smooth rock, Scotty—you wouldn't believe it!"

"Sure I would. Saw it last fall. Dad and I just stood there and laughed." He lowered his voice. "I'm going to be waiting my chance to dump Sue into it."

"Scot? That famous mine? Is it around here any-where?"

"No." He stood back and perched one foot on a rock. "Well, that was easy to say, but who knows *where* the mine is? If someone knew, they'd go after it."

"Isn't it a little bit dangerous for us to be here?"

"All the accidents have happened up nearer the Weaver's Needle. Dad and I hunted in this area and no one bothered us." Scotty's freckles hid in a sud-den grin. "It would be kind of great to get my teeth into another mystery." He posed and took on an air of fearlessness and aloofness. "You know, sounds in the night—rockslides, gunshots!"

Danny hunched his back and walked away. "Those things *have happened* already."

"Not here. Not on this side of the Superstitions. Dad would never bring Mom and Sue here if it wasn't safe. But," he added, lowering his voice and glancing toward his parents, "I'd like to do some browsing around—you know, where that mine is concerned."

Danny's grin shot into position. He came back and suddenly got interested in helping Scotty unpack the rest of the pans. "It's a cool idea. Not that we'd ever find it. But we could follow some of the clues, couldn't we? I mean, like the Weaver's Needle and the Sombrero?"

Scotty looked up toward the great rock formation that looked like a weaver's needle. "They say that the only people who've been killed in these mountains are those carrying picks and shovels," he mused aloud.

Danny thrust out his lower lip and nodded. "Sure! Because someone doesn't want that old mine to be found! But, you know, Scot—" He tugged at his lower lip with his teeth, pondering. "I really don't know as much about the Lost Dutchman Mine as you do."

"Well, the dozens of people who have been killed in these mountains were real enough! Rockslides during the night; shots in the back; rocks dropped from above. There have been as many as two and three killed in a party." He moved away from the grill to gather twigs for the fire. "But *who* does it? And why? Seems like anyone would have a right to find the mine and its gold."

"You still haven't told me anything about the mine," Danny reminded.

"Dad will have to fill you in," Scotty said, dumping an armload of small sticks on the fire site. "He knows a lot more about it than I do."

Night fell swiftly in the little valley. True to his word, Scotty took his mother back to the crest of the hill to show her the world sprawled at their feet. A thin mist of lights could be seen away in the distance. "That's part of Phoenix way over there, Mom." The cold mountain breeze billowed his shirt and he shivered. "We're a long way from civilization!"

"It's hard to believe we came so far. I didn't think that little jeep could crawl so high." She, too, shivered, and Scotty walked her back down the hill.

Scotty kind of liked the halo that the moon painted over her head. He liked her with the stars in her eyes. So good to be here on this high, windswept hill with his mother. Good to be in the valley with his family. Oh, it was going to be the greatest week ever!

"I guess we couldn't have made it if Dad and I hadn't found that old trail last fall."

The last glow of color dropped out of the sky, leaving only the blazing stars and the silver moon. They sat down with the others beside the campfire. Their bedrolls were laid neatly side by side on the sand, and the food supplies had been stashed away in a big plastic bag. Only a few fried potatoes remained in the skillet on the stove.

Beyond the rushing laughter of the water was the melancholy song of crickets and, occasionally, the wail of a coyote on yonder ridge. That savage cry dropped down into the valley and chilled the bones. Though every one of them had heard that cry for years, it never failed to pierce both body and mind.

Scotty scooted back from the fire a little. "Dad? Would you tell Danny the story of old Jakob Van Loon? I'd like to hear it again myself."

Mr. Hanson looked up sharply. He didn't have his Western hat on now and his hair was ruffled and windblown. His hands, calloused from hard work, wrapped about his knees. He began to speak thoughtfully.

"Well, it began with this man from Holland by the name of Jakob Van Loon. He was a miner who found this rich vein of gold here in the Superstitions. Many times the man would take his burro and go into Phoenix, and there he'd drop hints to various people as to the whereabouts of this gold mine.

"For instance, he'd tell how the sun would shine into the mouth of his cave in late afternoon and how he could see the old Military Trail from there. Men were always trying to follow him back to the mine, but he always lost them in the mountains."

"Is that all the story?" Danny asked, his brows furrowed in disappointment.

"Far from it." Mr. Hanson laid another log on the fire and then sat back cross-legged. "There's a fork in the mountains that's called the Fork of Randolf and Frazer Canyons. There's an old stone house at that point, and after climbing a short distance from that stone house one can see the rock formation the Weaver's Needle. The Needle is another clue." He paused, frowned as though some memory disturbed him, and then continued. "I suppose one most important clue is the face that looks down upon the canyons when the sun is shining just right. It's not a rock face, but a face that is produced merely by the shadows cast by the sun.

"Then, of course, right near the mine is a grave. If anyone finds the grave, he'll likely find the gold too."

Scotty looked up quickly. He hadn't heard about the grave. "Who is buried there, Dad?"

"A man by the name of Jacob Wisner, who was killed at the mine site and buried there. You see," Mr. Hanson said softly, "one of the best friends I ever had, went looking for the mine ten years ago. He made it as far as the grave and was shot in the head. It was weeks before we knew for certain that something was wrong. He was found by rangers and brought back for burial by helicopter."

"Oh. I didn't know about that either, Dad."

The brush on the hill was rustled by some animal; then, breaking the stillness of the moment, it seemed that every coyote in the Superstitions was bent upon sending a low, eerie howl toward the moon.

"What about the Sombrero?" Danny questioned at last. The youth was sitting forward, catching every word that was spoken. He was totally unaware of his dirty T-shirt and disheveled hair.

"Some folk think the Sombrero is a clue, but I doubt it. It's the Weaver's Needle that the old Dutchman always spoke about."

Scotty couldn't hold it back. "And when the moon is full, old Jakob Van Loon is supposed to circle Superstition Mountain. They say sometimes he laughs his wild, shrieking laugh, and sometimes he even shoots his rifle!"

Susan, who had been absorbing the story while letting her feet trail in the stream, now suddenly looked back over her shoulder through the trees. Then she cautiously made her way to her mother's side, her blue eyes frightened and angry. "Stop it, Scot! I don't think that was one bit funny!"

Scotty rolled with laughter. "Don't worry, Sue. Old Van Loon couldn't be doing anything but faking it out!"

"Scotty!"

He held out a hand, but he was still laughing inside. "OK, OK. But just remember, when Danny and I are finding all sorts of clues about this mine, don't you come trying to get in on the excitement." It would never happen and he knew it, but he couldn't help throwing it in.

Mr. Hanson slipped a New Testament from his shirt pocket. "I think we'd better have devotions and

turn in. He looked at Scotty and wrinkled his forehead. "Maybe we'd better read from I John on the
subject of brotherly love."

They were all awake, however, long after devotions, though no one spoke. They all stretched out
in their bedrolls and lay gazing up at the stars. Listening to the splash and rush of water—and to the
coyotes around their camp. And then, one by one,
they fell asleep.

2

DO COYOTES TAKE RADIOS?

CAMP WAS BUSTLING with sound and activity. Mr. Hanson was cleaning his 30-30 Winchester while listening to the news on the transistor radio.

Susan was getting the plastic container of margarine and eggs from the tiny little cave near the waterfall. It was cool there and things would keep fresh. Scotty had put a crude lattice made from grass and twigs in front of it the night before in hopes that no wild animals would get to the food.

Scotty picked up the frying pan and headed for the stream. "Looks like you were right in leaving those fried potatoes in the skillet, Mom, because someone did get hungry and eat them, just like you said."

Danny shrugged from his position of tying a shoe. "It wasn't me. I fell apart when I hit that sleeping bag."

"Probably Susan," Scotty murmured, bending close to the stream and using sand as a scouring agent. "She eats all the time any more."

The last word was scarcely out of his mouth when a tennis shoe came against him and suddenly thrust him forward. Scotty made a wild scramble, throwing pan and all into the water. But all in vain. Half rising

15

to catch his balance, he fell headlong into the icy mountain stream.

Danny paused in the act of tying his other shoe and stared toward his friend. "What are you doing, Scot?"

Scotty let out a yell of anger and cold and indignation. Retrieving the skillet, he started after his sister. "What's the matter with you? You crazy or something?"

Susan stood her ground, nose in the air and lips firm. "I'm not going to spend a week with you constantly trying to scare me or talking about me behind my back!"

Scotty was scarlet. "Look what you've done to me! Just look!"

A slight tremor passed over Susan and her lips parted a little. "I am."

"My shoes! I'll be wearing wet shoes all day long. And my clothes!" He was shaking with cold. "Mom didn't bring *all* my clothes just for a camping trip, y'know."

"I know." Susan trembled again and she turned away quickly.

"Are you laughing at me?"

Susan was really shaking now and her face was buried in her hands. "If you could just see yourself!" And she bent double and laughed until there were tears flowing down her face. "Oh, you look so *funnee!*" And she went off again into peals of laughter.

Mr. Hanson rose to his feet, and he suddenly looked half again as tall. His big hands went into the pockets of his levis and he turned to face Scotty and Susan.

"Don't you two think that's about enough? We came here for some rest and some fun, not to see a wrestling match." He cocked his graying head to one side. "Maybe we'd better read I John again today."

Scotty let the frying pan fall slack at his side. A deep sigh escaped his lips. "Sorry, Dad."

Mr. Hanson didn't look the least bit grim, but there was a firm set to his jaw that Scotty knew well. "You don't owe *me* an apology."

He looked slowly toward Susan. The fight was all gone. He grinned. "You want to be friends?"

Susan was still snickering now and then and trying desperately not to. "Sure! I'm sorry, Scotty."

He nodded. "I'm sorry too. I must look a sight." He glanced toward his father. "Did *you* eat the potatoes, Dad?"

Mr. Hanson was in the act of turning back to his gun, but at this question he stopped quickly, turning with a frown. "Wha—what did you say?"

Scotty held up the skillet. "That's why Susan was so mad at me. I said she must have eaten the rest of the fried potatoes during the night."

Their father looked completely mystified. "Well, it wasn't me. I slept the whole night."

Danny took the skillet out of his friend's limp hand. "Why don't you change clothes? I'll clean the skillet."

Mrs. Hanson, who had the pancake batter ready and had been waiting for the skillet's return, now came over slowly. "Why all this fuss about someone eating the potatoes during the night?"

"They were gone this morning, Mom, and I was just trying to figure out who got out of bed to eat them."

Susan squirmed. "It wasn't *me*!"

Scotty's mother shrugged and laughed. "Why does it matter? If someone was hungry— That's why I left them."

"But no one *did* eat them," Scotty said doggedly. "That's the thing."

"Well, someone certainly did, because they were gone this morning!" Mrs. Hanson stroked back a straying lock of hair with the back of her hand.

Scotty's father roved the mountains with his eyes. "I'll tell you who ate them. These hills are full of hungry coyotes. And the way we slept last night, any one of them could have crept into camp and eaten them. You remember they were all around." He started toward the camping stove, sniffing eagerly at the aroma of maple syrup and hot pancakes. "Frankly, I'm as hungry as a coyote myself. Come on, gang!"

After breakfast was over Scotty and Danny left camp to poke around on their own. Scotty had even invited his sister, but she had nestled down with "a good book" beside the waterfall, and there they left her.

"Where to?" asked Danny.

Scotty stood high on a rock, hands in his back pockets, brown eyes scouting the mountains. Everything looked fascinating. That shadow that was cast against the rocks—was it a cave, perhaps? And the ledge away to the south, towering, inviting—but impossible to climb to.

Finally Scotty grasped a small ledge of rock and pulled his long body upward until he could stand and see over the canyons sprawled below. "Come this way, Danny, it looks real neat."

They climbed upward, ever upward. The compass told them that they were due east of camp. Besides, after having hunted this area with his father, Scotty was sure of his position.

They perched at last on a great boulder that looked out over the wild, rock-strewn canyons and deep ravines. Beyond them, green-brown hills rose up to meet the shaggy pinnacles of rock. Two great buzzards circled lazily, their wings unfolded in a giant span. Far in the distance a natural earthen reservoir sparkled in the late afternoon sunlight.

Danny stared up to the shining black buzzards. "Hope they're not waiting for us," he remarked.

Scotty hooked his thumbs just inside his pockets. "Makes you feel pretty small, doesn't it, being away up here like this."

"Uh-huh."

A breeze stirred and a moment later a wind began singing through the rabbit brush. Then it fell back and the silence closed in. No stillness like the stillness of the mountains when the birds were hushed and no wild animals broke brush.

"You were really mad at Sue this morning?" Danny watched his friend thoughtfully.

"She was bugging me real bad."

Danny flicked an ant from his knee. "You did start it, you know."

"Yeah. She's really OK. I wouldn't have cared if she had come with us today."

Danny grunted. It was warm on the big rock, and he leaned back comfortably. "Who do you think took the potatoes?"

Scotty groaned aloud. "Oh, not again! Look,

Danny, I've been all through that." He narrowed his eyes to slits. "A coyote ate them during the night. That's all."

The tone of his voice told Danny he'd better not press the subject. "Scotty?"

"Hmmm?"

"The old prospector is dead. So is his partner, the other Jacob. *Now!* Who killed all those people who came looking for the gold mine?"

"Beats me!"

"I sure don't believe in ghosts," Danny declared emphatically.

Scotty chuckled, but he didn't speak. His gaze was fastened upon the reservoir away in the distance, and his thoughts were sober, almost depressed. When a gopher wiggled its tail toward him and then leaped behind a rock, the boy failed to be amused.

"OK!" Danny stood up, stretched and looked back toward his friend. There was no twinkle in his blue eyes. "If you want to stay in this lousy mood, go ahead. But I'm not going to let it come off on me."

Scotty jerked his head up in surprise. "Sorry, Danny. Can you find your way back all right?"

Danny didn't reply. He leaped lightly to the big rock just below him, and a moment later he was completely out of sight.

Scotty was more miserable alone than he had been with Danny. What *was* the matter with him, anyway? Last night he'd angered Susan. This morning he could gladly have popped the frying pan over her blond head. As it was, his father had had to get after him. It had even been hard for him to apologize to his sister. And now Danny was peeved. Wow! What a record. He'd better stay on the good side of his mother!

There's more to it than that, he thought. *I haven't pleased the Lord and I'm feeling pretty bad about it.*

Scotty pressed back against the boulder and prayed softly. He lingered for some time. After his heart was light again, he looked at his watch. Four-thirty. Better get back.

He stood and sighed deeply. The way was clear again between him and the Lord Jesus. Oh, how good! Now if he could really square things with Danny and Susan, it would be great. Not much of a trick to that. When his heart was right with the Lord, everything else just kind of fell into place.

Carefully he made his way over the rocks and through the smaller canyons to camp. It was longer than he'd realized. By five-fifteen the little green valley with its sparkling falls and laughing stream appeared and Scotty stepped into the grass and walked down the hill.

"You're just in time," Mr. Hanson said, looking up from where he was cleaning a rabbit. "I need the radio to get the evening news."

"The radio?" Scotty stopped where he was. A frown of surprise fell across his forehead.

"We didn't take the radio," Danny broke in from his place by the stream.

Mr. Hanson looked blank. "But—where is it, then? There are only five of us here. Susan and your mother left camp for a while to poke around the hills and they didn't have it with them. I went rabbit hunting and I certainly didn't have it with me. That leaves you and Danny. One of you must have taken it and forgotten—"

Danny looked more than just blank. "I've never touched the radio, Mr. Hanson."

Scotty seemed to be reining himself in, as he would Rocky when he wanted to move unwisely. "Dad, I didn't take the radio."

The man scratched his ear thoughtfully. "Well! We finally decided that a brave coyote wandered in last night to eat fried potatoes." He laughed hoarsely. "But—do coyotes take radios?"

3

MUSIC AND A PONCHO

SCOTTY'S DARK EYES lifted but he didn't raise his head. Once he even opened his mouth to speak, but he closed it again without doing so. After all, the fried potatoes and coyote bit had gotten him into enough trouble. *Besides that,* he thought, *every time the Lord has forgiven me for something, the devil is right there trying to trip me up again. This time I'm not going to fall for it!*

He noticed that Danny was fingering his shirttail nervously. Maybe he had had it and something had happened and— Uh-uh. He wasn't going to think that way either.

His friend's blue gaze came up slowly to meet his. "Well?" Danny asked. "This is your big chance."

Scotty shook his head. "Maybe a coyote did take it."

Mr. Hanson took off his Western hat long enough to smooth back his crisp hair. "I don't blame you for feeling that way, son. It does look strange. Food missing this morning. Now the transistor." He replaced his hat and his piercing eyes searched out the little valley.

Scotty caught his father's thoughts. "You want us

to tramp through the grass, Dad, and see if we can come up with it?"

"I think that's a good idea." Mr. Hanson patted the camping table. "It was right here when our paths scattered this morning. When we all got back, Danny came from that direction." He pointed toward the mountains. "Susan and you, honey, came from the upper rim of the canyon; and I came in from the rear."

"And Scotty never took it!" Danny put in abruptly.

"I believe you," Scotty's father returned firmly. "OK. Let's check out the valley."

Scotty wondered vaguely how his dad expected the radio to be in the grass, or somewhere in the valley, if no one in the camp had touched it. But he said nothing.

However, as he and Danny walked along the left side of the lovely valley, they exchanged meaningful glances. Scotty lifted an eyebrow in perfect understanding, though neither of them had spoken.

Danny grinned and his teeth flashed white against his brown face. "Could be," he murmured.

"I don't see how, but it sure has all the earmarks."

Danny's grin grew wider. "Be kind of fun," he said, keeping his voice low.

Scotty squinted into the sun and his freckles dove into the creases. His face was eager with excitement. "Agreed! Another mystery would be too good to be true." He hesitated. "Only thing is, the last time *we* found the crooks. This time it might be that *he,* or *they,* have found us!"

Danny studied his friend's face. "What would anyone want with us?"

Scotty couldn't help saying it. "Maybe it's the old prospector guarding his gold." But he was laughing and Danny knew he wasn't serious.

"Nope." The sandy-haired youth shook his head. "This is a person—because he *eats*! And listens to music. If there's a mystery here at all, we're not dealing with a ghost!"

"Uhmm," Scotty shrugged. "We're probably just letting our imaginations roam anyhow."

"Susan probably was listening to it by the stream sometime today and dropped it in the water and she's afraid to tell."

Scotty poked his friend in the shoulder. "Watch it, or you'll be having the same problem I had this morning."

"Yeah, you sure did have a problem!" Danny agreed. "But you're OK now. What happened?"

Scotty took a deep breath. *"I prayed!"* he cried, only half laughing. "I couldn't even stand *myself*!"

The party of five tramped every foot of the valley, but no transistor radio appeared. They met back at camp together, empty-handed and with expressions of bewilderment.

"It's somewhere," Susan said, wiping the perspiration from her forehead, "but it's certainly not in the valley."

Silence fell over the little group. Each person was occupied with his and her own thoughts. Fried potatoes. A transistor radio. Just—gone.

At last Mr. Hanson lifted his face toward the mountains, and when he spoke it sounded as though he was trying to convince himself of his theory. "We'll have to throw out this animal idea. That's out! So it has to be a person." He spread his hands expressively. "And the only kind of people you ever find up in here are prospectors. And not many of them. I figure that a hungry prospector, away from civilization for some time, became hungry for something besides beans and pan-fried bread. He saw us come in and set up camp, smelled our food and waited his chance for a free morsel. Can't blame him, really."

"And the radio?" Susan pursued.

"Well, as I said, away from civilization for a long time would make a man thirsty for news. So the radio was the perfect answer."

"Dad?"

It was the first question Scotty had asked, and he was almost afraid to ask this. "If he was so thirsty for news, why didn't he just come to you and ask you?"

Mr. Hanson took a long, cool drink of water before answering. "Well, Scot, you've met prospectors before. You know how so many of them are. Maybe it's the sun—or loneliness—I don't know. They become queer after a while. This prospector is probably afraid of us." He heaved a great sigh. "Anyway, it's over and he's gone. Let's forget the whole thing and have a good time this week, all right?"

"Sure, Dad," Susan agreed.

Scotty twisted his mouth to one side and nodded doubtfully. "Sure, Dad."

Mrs. Hanson began to work around the table. "Well! After all this, the sun is going down and you must all be hungry. I'll have something ready in a little while. Scotty? Will you and Danny get the fire started?"

The tense feeling disappeared after a good meal. There were left only the chilly night and the star-splashed heavens. Tomorrow night the moon would be full and yellow, and the coyotes would come closer still and there would be the thrilling wildness in their call. And—

Scotty moved a little closer to the leaping flames of their campfire. All they needed tomorrow night was for the old Dutchman Jakob Van Loon to stand on yonder pinnacle and laugh his bloodcurdling laugh!

No. It would never happen. The potatoes and radio were good enough starters for a suspense story without adding the laughter of a dead man. And Scotty's heart couldn't wholeheartedly go along with his father's theory. Not that he was saying so!

Mr. Hanson read the Bible that night from Psalm 34. Whether he chose to read there on that special night, no one ever knew. Anyway, one certain verse brought great comfort that night to every heart: "The angel of the Lord encampeth round about them that fear him, and delivereth them."

"The Bible used to be a lot of words to me," Scotty mused aloud. "But it means more than that now." The lock of brown hair fell over his forehead and he didn't bother to shove it aside. "Right now it means God's voice, telling us that He has an angel camping with us and there's no need to fear."

Susan leaned forward and there was a look of mild surprise upon her face. "Say, that's right, Scotty! It does mean that. He *is* here! To keep us and to protect us from harm."

Danny pursed his lips and nodded. "Jesus promised, too, that He'd never leave us nor forsake us!"

"Why doesn't all of God's Word come alive that way?"

Mr. Hanson slapped his knee. "Because we fail to realize that it is the Word of God. God's letter, really, to the world. And not only that," he went on, "but the Bible comes to life and becomes alive in the heart only when the Holy Spirit quickens it to us. Maybe we all should get into the habit of asking the Holy Spirit to make the Word of God real and living."

There was silence for a time. Then the moon slipped easily and quietly over the jagged pinnacles of rock to the east, to bathe the Superstition Mountains with its white-yellow glow.

The response was almost immediate. A coyote howled so close to the valley that, for a moment, the camping party thought it was *in* the valley. A resounding cry came from the opposite side of the valley, and the group waited with bated breath as one animal crept down through the grass away behind them, to make its way to its mate. After that a chorus of weird and lonely cries was sent toward the heavens.

"Why do they do it?" Susan asked softly.

"That's one of the mysteries of nature, I guess. Several times while I've been hunting, and the moon has been full, they've come right up to my camp. I've even had them scratch on the canvas of my pup tent." Mr. Hanson paused as an eerie *yap, yap, yee-oow!* rose and fell again. "It's as if they have more courage when the moon is full."

Suddenly another sound mingled with the cries of the wild beasts. The group was slow in realizing just what the other sound was; but as soon as it gripped

them, a sense of great wonderment fell upon each one.
Music.

"Music?" Susan whispered, stricken.

Music. Away—somewhere. Music that drove the
coyotes to a chorus of throaty noises, and then to dis-
cordant howls. Music! It seemed to come from no-
where in particular, and yet it was everywhere.

"My radio," Mr. Hanson whispered hoarsely. "It
has to be!"

"Maybe one of them took it after all," Danny
grinned. "They certainly seem to be enjoying it."

"I think it's really hurting their ears," Mrs. Hanson
put in. She put her hand in Mr. Hanson's. "It must
have been some old prospector after all."

Scotty glanced at his father. Only one thing wrong
with that thought. Prospectors, at least old ones, went
to bed around dusk and rose again at the crack of
daylight. So, unless this one was completely looney—
if it *was* a prospector—he ought to have been asleep
hours ago.

"We may never know," Mr. Hanson replied at last
to his wife's statement. He forced himself to stir.
"Anyway, let's turn in. I think I've found myself a
beautiful spot for calling in coyotes and bobcats. Early
this afternoon I used the rabbit caller and called in a
deer instead!"

"Honest, Mr. Hanson?" But it was a flat question.
There was no eagerness or enthusiasm in Danny's
voice. He said it because it was something to say.
Danny was uneasy about the music, and talking
helped.

Mr. Hanson took off his wide-brimmed hat and
hung it over a forked branch from a palo verde tree.

"Why don't you boys come with me tomorrow? It could turn out to be quite exciting."

Danny pulled off his boots slowly, slipped off his socks and stuck his feet into the water. There was a light in his eyes that the dying coals of the fire hadn't placed there. "Looks like we're getting enough excitement right here at camp. Who knows what's going to happen tomorrow?"

Scotty had said nothing during the whole conversation. Neither had Susan, except for the one hoarse whisper about the music. They were sitting close together, exchanging a glance now and then, but for the most part just listening to the wild cries of the slinking coyotes as they moved close to their camp and to the music higher in the mountains. Such a strange night. One that tasted of danger and suspense and intense drama.

Sleep did not come easily that night. Scotty was started to wakefulness over and over by sounds near camp. A snapping twig. The sudden chorus of crickets. A breeze that caused a pan to move slightly on the grill. Disturbing dreams of old prospectors leading donkeys whose backs were loaded with flour and cornmeal and salt and coffee. One old prospector— Jakob Van Loon. A mine that held a secret ledge of pure, virgin gold—gold that was hidden from the—

"Wha— What? What's the matter?"

"Don't get bent outta shape!" Danny grinned. "It's time to roll out, didn't you know?"

Scotty's brain began to cooperate slowly. Get up? "I just went to bed!"

"I know. And if I'd had the kind of night you did,

I think I'd be awfully glad someone was kind enough to wake me."

Scotty unzipped his sleeping bag and sat up, fingers tangled through his dark hair. "You're so right! I was just at this moment on my way to the gold mine with Jakob Van Loon, and I think he was going to kill me. Wow! What a night!"

"Your dad ate breakfast early and headed for his 'beautiful spot.' He said for your mother not to worry, it's a place where he can keep an eye on the canyon. Besides, she's going to join him after we've all had breakfast." Danny scooted a little nearer and nudged Scotty. "Hey, Scot, I didn't know your mother could handle a gun and liked to target practice on coyotes."

Scotty pressed his lips and nodded. "Best shootin' woman in the West!" he boasted with a laugh. "What are we having for breakfast?"

"Bacon and eggs." When Scotty would have moved to fold up his sleeping bag, Danny put a hand on his arm. "Say, where would you say that music from the radio came from last night?"

Scotty shrugged and his brown eyes narrowed in a frown. He made a gesture to a point above and in front of them. "Up there somewhere. Up in those crags maybe. I'm not sure."

Danny nodded in agreement. "That's what Susan thinks too."

Scotty cocked his head and paused, sleeping bag only half rolled up. "Where does Sue fit in?"

Danny stroked his sandy hair thoughtfully. "Well, uh— we— that is, *she* thought it would be a good idea for her to come along with us. She doesn't want to call coyotes and she can't stay in camp alone with all that's been going on. You know," he ended limply.

Scotty snapped his sleeping bag neatly into place and put it at the base of a cottonwood tree with the others. "Well, I guess Susan won't be too much trouble. And I'd like to check out that music too."

Scotty was the last one to eat that morning and he washed his own eating utensils while his mother checked her rifle. They had brought paper plates to eat from so they could dispose of them. Scotty felt pretty good about that.

"All set, Mother? We won't leave camp till you're ready to meet Dad."

She flashed him a smile, and her blue eyes shone. "I *am* ready. You three have a good morning, but—be careful."

"Right, Mom!"

Scotty watched as his mother strode from the valley and began to make her way up the mountain. Kind of funny to watch her—all feminine and graceful one minute, and marching away with a rifle flung over her shoulder the next. She could sure wallop a deer too! Scotty had seen her do it. Well—!

"I thought you'd decided to stay here," Danny teased.

"If you don't hurry, I'm going to beat both of you!" Susan challenged. She was off with a bound, wiry and energetic. She wore tennis shoes instead of boots, and the rubber soles clung steadfastly to the rocks, as she leaped from one to another.

The two boys scrambled up behind her. It seemed as easy to bolt up the mountain as it was for the great buck that broke from the brushy hillside ahead of them and darted away. When they paused at last, however, they were trembling and gasping for breath.

"Look!" Susan panted, holding her stomach. "Look how far we've come."

"Even our valley has disappeared." Scotty squinted toward the jagged pinnacles of rock still far ahead of them. "Do you still think that's where the music came from?"

Susan shrugged. "How can anyone be sure? It seemed to come from all over last night. But — I thought it centered from up there."

"Yeah," Danny grunted. He stood with one foot braced against a rock and his thumbs hooked inside his pockets. "The mountains can really fool a person at night."

They waited a few minutes longer, while their breathing returned to normal and the quivering left their legs. Scotty had brought a small canteen along, and they each took a sip of water.

So still this morning. Not even a mountain sparrow lent its song to the lonely canyons and windswept crags. Not a gopher came out of its hole to play. Nor a rabbit from its burrow. The only movement was that of a giant, spiraling dust-devil away in the valley below, announcing that spring had come. But the whirling of its wind did not reach them there. And then, in the very silence about them, there was indeed a sound. Very small at first— Lingering.

The three young people whirled to face one another, to be certain the others heard it too.

"Scot—"

"Shhh!" Scotty listened intently. "That— Don't you know what it is?" he whispered.

Danny bared his teeth and nodded. "The radio!"

It was playing rock and roll. The harsh, jazzed-up kind. And the sounds fell from a point above them.

Their eyes all questioned each other. *Who?* What kind of person were they dealing with? And why had he taken the radio?

"Dad must have been right," Susan said quietly. "It must be some old crank of a prospector."

Scotty made signs for silence, and then he began to climb, more cautiously this time. When his boots slipped on the shaly mountainside, he paused fairly long before continuing. The others followed close behind. The music was clearer now, but it was the only sound in the mountains. They could not even hear Mr. Hanson's coyote caller squeaking like a wounded rabbit in order to lure the coyotes in. There was only the radio and their own fast-beating hearts.

Suddenly Scotty came to a sharp crest of a hill and stopped again. From the sound of the radio, he knew that whoever had taken it was just over that crest.

Better go back, he thought. *Better get Dad and— But how would we ever find this place again? Just a—quick look and—"*

He eased his head up just high enough to look over the crest. But what he saw only mystified him further. It wasn't a canyon on the other side at all, just a little dip where a great cluster of rocks and boulders cradled a spot of lush grass. But this grass had been pressed to the earth, so that now it looked like a place where a bear or a deer might hole up. Only it wasn't. It wasn't, because there was the radio sitting on a rock playing rock and roll. And beside it was a poncho such as a Mexican or an Indian might wear.

Scotty became acutely breathless and his eyes were wide and searching. Could he dash over there, grab up the radio and dash back again? Did he dare? There was no one in sight. On the other side of the boulders grew masses of tall, sharp bear grass. Whoever stayed here would have to come through that bear grass first!

Slowly he brought his body into a hard ball and then into a full crouch. He motioned for Susan and Danny to stay where they were. Crawling over the top of the sharp hill, he sprang lightly to the radio. He felt angry that this kind of music came from his father's radio, but he dared not move the dial or turn it off.

On further thought, Scotty grabbed up the poncho, stuck it under one arm and headed back for the side of the hill. He never saw the pair of black, tormented eyes that watched his every move from beyond the bear grass.

4

THE APACHE CURSE

ONCE OVER THE SIDE of the hill, Scotty motioned
frantically for Danny and Susan to scram. They did,
slipping and sliding, for this particular area held a
lot of loose rock.

As Scotty got farther and farther away from the
strange "bedding down place"—he didn't know what
else to call it—he turned the radio lower. Finally he
turned it off completely. There was an almost overwhelming sense of danger and Scotty prayed for safety
for all three of them.

Only when the trio had dropped far below and
were huddled together under a great ledge of rock
did they stop long enough to sip again from the canteen and try to breathe normally again.

"Who—wh—who was it?" Susan stammered.

Scotty shook his head. "I didn't see anyone at all!
Let's get on back to camp."

"But, Scot—"

The dark-haired youth laid a finger across his lips.
"Later!" he murmured.

A breeze stirred and Scotty was suddenly taken
back with a strange odor. He grimaced. Wha— The
poncho? Oh, sure! It was heavy wool and extremely
dirty, smelling of perspiration and old smoke. Who-

ever wore this poncho had to be a person who couldn't care less about cleanliness.

Down over the last great boulders, the trio reached the valley at last. Through the ankle-deep grass and around the camping table they walked, never stopping until they had pulled off shoes and socks and eased their feet into the icy water.

Once that was done, however, Danny wasted no time. "OK, Scot, let's hear all about it. What did you see? Were there other things there besides the radio and poncho?" He reached for the poncho, studied the ground-in dirt, finally sniffed it and muttered, "Ugh! I wish I hadn't done that."

Susan wouldn't even touch it. She looked at the garment critically, noting the worn fringe along the neckline and along the hem. "Probably at one time it was a beautiful poncho." There was a moment of hesitation, and then, "Scotty? Indians wear ponchos, don't they? Not—not *prospectors*?"

Scotty furrowed his forehead. "Mexicans too, especially the true Spanish Americans down in Mexico. But I'm with you, Sis—not prospectors." He took two handfuls of the cold mountain water and splashed it on his face and neck. "You asked me what I saw, Danny? I saw exactly what you see right here. A poncho and Dad's missing radio. They were right there in a little grassy spot where the *person* has been staying. I could tell, because the grass was all mashed down. And it was almost completely closed in by rocks and bear grass.

Susan leaned back against the base of the cottonwood tree, listening for a moment to the breeze singing in the branches. "How could anyone live up there without food and water? *In the rocks?* I just can't understand that."

Danny tossed his sandy head. "How do you know there isn't another spring up where he is? And, as for food— We know for certain that he had fried potatoes night before last."

"But why? Why would anyone want to hide up there in the rocks? And don't say it's likely to be an Indian or a Mexican looking for the gold, because I just can't feature them playing American rock and roll for enjoyment."

"Right!" Scotty admitted quickly. "So you're just where I am, Susan. No answer. Just—no answer."

Danny looked away to the crags of rock and nodded again. No answer to this mystery. Scotty was sure right about that.

A sound brought the three of them to their feet. But a moment later they sighed in relief and sat back down, dropping their feet into the water with a bigger splash than they intended to make.

"Dad! Mom! Come take a look at a hard day's work."

Mr. Hanson pushed back his hat with a thumb. After ejecting the shells, he placed the rifle carefully to one side. "Talk about a hard day's work! We called in five coyotes, two deer—by mistake—and one bobcat that was—" He broke off, seeing his radio back where it belonged. "Where did you find this?" He picked up the transistor and tested it.

"Works great, Dad! The music led us righ' 'o it. And this!" Triumphantly he held up the filthy poncho.

It was the poncho that Mr. Hanson reach d for then. A look of deep concern crossed his face. He examined and reexamined the smelly garment. His eyes seemed very dark as he scanned the pinnacles in front of and above their camp.

"That's where they were, Dad," Susan said quickly. "Up there in a grassy place where it looked like an animal had bedded down during the day. The poncho was draped over a rock and the radio was there too."

Scotty tossed her a look. "Susan wasn't even there," he protested. "But she did give a pretty good play-by-play description of what was there, all right."

Mr. Hanson pondered. "And no one in sight?"

"That's right, Dad."

There was a long silence, in which the man stooped to reexamine the poncho. Clearly he saw that the patterns of the one-time beautiful poncho were those of the Apache. After a minute or two he laid it aside; but his countenance was disturbed.

"Could you take me there again, Scotty?" he asked quietly at last.

Scotty looked startled. There was a sudden stirring of excitement, even while his heart sagged at the thought of it. "Why—sure, Dad! At least, I think I can. But—why?"

"Because we have to return this poncho."

Scotty's face twisted. "You mean because you think I stole it?"

The six-foot-two man at his side didn't answer immediately. "Danny, stay here and keep your eyes open." He gestured. "Might keep that rifle loaded."

It was three o'clock in the afternoon. They couldn't possibly make the round trip in less than two and a half hours. Scotty groaned inwardly. He had blisters on his feet now. Just a second. He pulled off his boots and replaced them with his tennis shoes. He might come home with burrs in his feet, but at least tennis shoes would make it easier walking for now.

They checked their canteens and tucked some sandwiches into a plastic bag to carry along. But when they were about to leave the tiny valley, Scotty's mother followed them.

Her eyes were gently imploring. "Do you have to go? Is it *really* so important?"

Mr. Hanson put his big arm around her and, in spite of her jeans and trim figure, she seemed suddenly very insecure, very helpless.

"You'll be all right. And we'll make it as fast as we can." He spread his arms wide. "Look! Nothing bad has really happened at all. Some character in these mountains simply got hungry our first night and came and got some food. Code of the Superstitions!" he laughed. "Hungry? Eat! Besides," he added soberly, "this poncho doesn't belong to us, and it gets cold in the mountains at night. We wouldn't want to make some Apache freeze, would we?"

"Of course not," she smiled. But the word *Apache* had stuck in her mind, and they saw her walk back to camp very deep in thought.

Scotty did not speak to his father until they were some distance from camp. "What makes you so sure it's an Apache Indian, Dad?"

"The colors. The pattern. Even the way it's made. It's Apache, all right."

"Dad?" Scotty ducked the thorny arms of a mesquite tree and at the same moment brushed his leg against a piece of catclaw. "Ouch! Dad, why? What would an Apache be doing up here? And why would he want to play rock and roll?"

Mr. Hanson crawled up a difficult slope after his son. "Most Indians are so Americanized today that they do whatever the white man does. You should know that!"

"But why would he be here in the first place?" Scotty insisted.

The man reached the summit of a hill and paused to rest. Sitting in a little grassy place, he plucked a long stem of grass and stuck it in his mouth. "All right, Scot. I'm going to tell you a legend about this lost gold mine. The one old Jakob Van Loon found and mined for himself."

Scotty waited. He'd had the feeling all along that the story hadn't been complete. He'd never been satisfied with all the explanations.

"Sometime along the way the old Spanish Rialto Mines began to come into being here in these mountains. They were worked for a number of years. Along this same period of time, apparently after the death of Jakob Van Loon in the home of a Negress in the Indian village of Phoenix, the Apaches gained or regained control of the mine. The gold was so pure that it didn't have to be processed or smelted but could be shipped directly to the mint. *This*," he emphasized, "is nothing more or less than history."

"Wow!"

"The legend, however, tells of a curse the Apaches put on the white man where that mine is concerned."

Scotty leaned forward eagerly, his brown eyes aglow over the thrilling story. "Go on, Dad," he urged.

"Well, I never said much about it because I thought

it was all legendary. But the story goes that any white man who comes looking for the mine will meet with sudden, violent death — and you know from countless newspaper stories that that's exactly what has happened through the years.

"For instance, Scot— And this is also history! Several times when the Apaches have had great needs on the reservation, the Indian men have suddenly appeared with vast quantities of gold. And when they return to the reservation, they go with new pickup trucks, cattle, sheep and horses to replenish their herds and flocks."

"Then it's the Apaches who do the killings?"

His father grinned but there wasn't any real humor in it. "I don't say that, Scot, because I've never been on the scene. But this *is* an Apache poncho, and I think we ought to get it back."

5

JAKOB VAN LOON
LAUGHS AGAIN

"WHY DID THE APACHES ever come here?"

"They used to live here—now they're on the San Carlos Indian Reservation. They still come here every year for some sort of ceremonies."

"And they know where the gold is—" Scotty mused aloud, frowning. "I guess they must still be here, some of them." He gave his father a half smile. "Well, would you believe *one*? With a poncho? Maybe they guard the mine, or something?"

"If this is so, then we must be a lot closer to the old Dutchman's mine than we dream!"

"Yeah," the youth breathed softly. "What's the clue nearest the mine, Dad?"

"The grave of Jacob Wisner, Jakob Van Loon's partner. There's a saying Van Loon left behind, along with his clues: 'Find the grave of Jacob Wisner and you have found the mine.' And don't you go getting ideas into your head!"

Scotty fell silent. His rubber-soled shoes took him easily upward over the boulders, but he missed digging his bootheels into the shaly rock to keep from sliding.

"Dad, that must be why no one has hurt us up here. We don't have picks or shovels with us, and that Apache must know that we aren't here to look for gold."

"That's the way I figure it too," his father agreed. "It also makes sense why others have met with death —if there are guards here who see some men getting too close to the mine."

Scotty stopped and took a few deep breaths. The wind had risen and was singing through the ocotillo. It felt cool too, blowing their shirts and their perspiring faces. In another hour it would be sharper, however, and with a definite chill in it. They must hurry.

Suddenly Scotty stopped again. "Dad, I think this is the place! Closer than I thought. Let me go ahead and see."

Mr. Hanson caught his son's ankle. "Wait! Let me go first, and you can come behind me. Here—give me the poncho."

"OK. But careful, Dad," Scotty whispered. "It's just over the crest here."

The man seemed to be holding his breath as he stretched his long frame toward the crest of the hill. After a moment he nodded and gave the heavy poncho a toss that landed it square on the grass. Then, ducking swiftly back, the two began again to make their way down the steep slope.

Scotty waited until they were some distance away before asking, "No one in sight, Dad?"

"No one. But when the Indian who owns the poncho sees that we have returned it, he'll understand that we are not his enemy." He chuckled under his breath. "Maybe he'll even make an attempt to return our food!"

Scotty lifted an eyebrow. "You know what? I wouldn't count on that."

The sun was already out of sight as the two dipped down into a canyon. And, as soon as the sunlight left these canyons, it immediately became chilly. An air of gloom seemed to have settled here this late afternoon, and from now on it would rapidly grow dark. Already a fox had crept from its burrow and was making its lonely way through the brush opposite them.

"About the curse, Dad. Are you going to say anything about it to the others?"

Mr. Hanson climbed onto a ledge of rock and extended his hand for Scotty. "No, I don't plan to, Scotty. As a matter of fact, if anything else happens, I'm going to pull out and we'll wind things up at Canyon Lake."

They reached camp just as the sun slid over the rim of the little valley and it too was plunged into shade and coolness. The aroma of freshly perked coffee and of ham sizzling in the skillet drifted lazily to Scotty and his father, and they hastened their steps toward the table.

Mrs. Hanson's perpetual smile played about her lips. "Did you get the poncho back without trouble?"

"Sure did, honey." Her husband sniffed. "Smells terrific, and we're two hungry people!"

"We were waiting for you." She lifted the lid from the skillet, disclosing great slices of browned ham and potatoes. "There for a minute I was afraid to cook potatoes!" she confessed.

Scotty and his father exchanged glances so quickly that no one noticed. But everyone laughed and the group felt suddenly free and gay. They were even able to joke their way through the evening meal, and Scotty felt certain that all tenseness was over and there would be no further surprises or mysteries.

The stars burst out one by one, until the black, black sky was ablaze with silver. The moon that night was bigger than ever. Orange-yellow, it lay over the crags of rock like a lazy pumpkin.

Scotty was awake for a time. He smiled at his father's usual wrestling with his sleeping bag.

"This thing wasn't made for a man as tall as me!"

Scotty had heard him say it dozens of times.

Quiet descended. Then there was a sound by the grill and a pan was moved gently. Mr. Hanson tore out of the sleeping bag that gave him such trouble and grabbed his gun.

At the sound, however, two black noses lifted quickly, and feet that were swifter than those of any athlete suddenly bounded out of the valley and back into the brown-green hills. It had only been a couple of deer, lured into the valley by the smell of bacon grease.

With a grunt, the man settled back into his sleeping bag and again took up the struggle of making his tall frame fit into it. Fifteen minutes later his breathing grew heavy and relaxed, and in another minute he was snoring lightly.

An hour passed by. Everyone was asleep but Scotty. The fire had died out until there were only a few red coals left in the ashes. A breeze had come up, sweeping gently into the valley. It stirred the giant cottonwood tree beside the bubbling stream until it seemed that the entire valley was alive with strange gurglings and endless laughter.

Scotty studied the stars and watched as the moon crept slowly across the heavens. There was a stirring in his heart tonight. Such odd things happening— A person out there somewhere who stole food and radios and wore a poncho. An Apache. Why was he here, really? Were they that close to the mine? Where was this Indian right now? Was he truly innocent of intending them harm? Or could he be ruthless, dangerous, if any one of them stumbled a little too near the Lost Dutchman Mine?

"The angel of the LORD encampeth round about them that fear him, and delivereth them." Scotty softly mouthed the words. He *did* believe that, didn't he? *I'm sure I believe it, Lord,* he said within his heart. His faith had been tested when he and Danny had found themselves shut in that cave with the men who had the talking doll,[1] hadn't it? Then God would keep them all again this time. *Father, if I'm going to be a missionary some day, I'm sure my faith must be tested many times. Only—don't ever let me fail You! I wouldn't want to do that!*

The wind was growing stronger, and once lightning flashed through the sky, followed by a clap of thunder. Scotty wondered vaguely where they would bed down if a storm *did* come. No big caves in this valley. Oh, well!

One by one the stars were disappearing; but the

---

[1] Read *Scotty and the Mysterious Message.*

moon, hidden a moment ago by a dark thundercloud, now sailed serenely into full view again. A strange feeling came over Scotty and he found himself propped on an elbow so he coud look around their camp. No one there.

And then suddenly something happened. There came the sound of laughter. Deep, mocking laughter that rang down from the ridge above them and echoed and reechoed through the hills.

"Dad!"

"Shhh! I hear it, Susan!"

The wind hushed its whining and laughing, and there was only the gurgling stream and the wild laughter. Then there was a snap as Mr. Hanson slipped a shell into his rifle and closed the breach.

A full moon! Jakob Van Loon! *When the moon is full, Van Loon walks the Superstitions again, and sometimes his laughter can be heard in the mountains.*

6

A HIPPIE?

THE SWATH OF DARK CLOUDS moved silently beneath the great yellow moon, concealing it completely. Again lightning split the heavens in two, followed by a mighty roll of thunder. And the laughter of the madman was put to silence.

The wind stirred the treetops again and a coyote cried, and very slowly the storm passed on without striking that part of the mountains.

The five people in the valley were all sitting straight up in their sleeping bags. Susan was shivering and trying to talk, but her words came out in such a torrent that they made little sense.

Mr. Hanson was in a half crouch, rifle cradled in his arms. When he spoke, his voice was low and commanding. "Now, we don't believe that dead men walk, so forget that. What we heard came from our Indian friend or from some wild animal. I suspect that we are close to the gold mine and the Apache is trying to carry through with the superstition of the laughter in order to frighten us away."

Scotty's mother scooted closer to her husband. "You said 'Apache' when you left to return the poncho," she said quietly, but with a little tremor in her voice. "Now you said it again. Are there Apaches on the mountain with us?"

"Well, I suspect there is one. I don't know about any others—and I haven't even seen *one*!" He hesitated. "But that poncho was definitely Apache weave and pattern."

Danny tried to keep the shiver out of his voice. "Why would an Apache be here?"

Mr. Hanson rose and sat on a rock beside them. "I can't answer that, because I can't be sure. Try and go back to sleep. I'm just going to sit here for a while and keep an eye on things. We'll pull out tomorrow and go to the lake for a day or two."

"I'll buy that!" Susan chimed.

"I'm afraid I will too," her mother agreed. "The incidents weren't too bad until tonight." She hesitated and whispered to her husband, "I've never heard laughter like that!"

"Weird, all right. But try not to worry about it. Good night, honey."

No one slept much the rest of the night. Now and then someone would drop off, but there was a restlessness now that kept anyone from sleeping soundly. As soon as the pale gray and pink of dawn began to light up the sky, everyone began to stir. There was security just in being awake and able to be up and moving about.

"What time are we going to pull out?" Scotty asked, moving to his father in the half light.

His dad squinted at the sky. "Well, things always seem better in the daylight, you know. Maybe your mother and I will bring in a few rabbits for lunch, and then we'll leave."

"You're right, Dad," Susan murmured softly. "Everything does seem different now that it's getting light. Last night—the laughter—why, it's almost like a dream now! But," she added, "I'm afraid I'll remember how it was when night falls again."

Mrs. Hanson, standing beside the camping table, looked back toward her family with an expression of bewilderment. "Where did we put the ham last night?"

Scotty thought for a minute and then gestured toward the falls. "In our little cave, maybe? I'll see." And, before his mother could reply, he was off with a bound.

"It's not there!" Susan called loudly. She turned to her mother excitedly. "There was just enough left for breakfast, and I knew it would keep all night, because it gets so cold. I wrapped it in foil and put it right—"But here her words went dangling into nothingness.

"It isn't here," Mrs. Hanson said quietly.

Mr. Hanson and Danny took over the search, but they both knew it was useless. A piece of ham didn't walk off a table. Neither could a piece of silver foil be successfully hidden anywhere around the table. The ham was gone. And Scotty, returning from the little cave with the butter and canned milk, shook his head.

Susan was staring at her father wide-eyed. "Coyote, Dad?"

It broke the spell and they laughed nervously together.

"No. Not a coyote." Mr. Hanson's face was much perplexed. "Our Apache friend. It could be no one else." He gazed toward the crags of rock towering above them. "He must be either totally mad or lost. Or—both. If he were a guard, he would be supplied with food. I can't imagine what's going on."

"Are we still going to wait until this afternoon to pack up and leave?" Danny questioned, his brows drawn into a **V** at his nose.

Scotty stood frowning, thumbs hooked into his back pockets and a look of dismay on his freckled face. Boy, he sure hated to walk off and leave a good mystery behind him!

Mr. Hanson didn't answer right away. He started a low fire in the grill so the coals would be just right when his wife wanted to start the hot cakes. Then he turned slowly, reached for his hat and finally spoke. "The Indian never bothers anything during the daytime. Except for the radio, that is. He comes for food during the night. He's really a hard one to figure." The man leaned back against the trunk of a cottonwood and sighed. "He's never made any attempt to hurt anyone, that's for certain. Yet—that wild laugh last night was the laugh of a madman. And a madman, whether Indian or white, cannot be trusted." He nodded as though to himself. "Your mother and I will go out as soon as breakfast is over. This is the best time of day to get rabbits anyway. We'll just skirt the valley—"

"There are plenty of cottontails around this valley, Dad, because of the water and all."

"I know it. We've seen a dozen already."

"Then we'll stay here and get things packed and ready," Susan offered.

Mr. Hanson reached for his small .32 revolver,

checked it and handed it to Scotty. "And you take this, son. If anything out of the ordinary takes place, just shoot into the air three times. OK?"

"Right, Dad!"

The three young people didn't move too enthusiastically, however. Now that the sun was coming up and the valley was decked with light and the stream was murmuring so joyously, they hated to leave. Even the birds were singing this morning, bouncing from bough to bough and twittering with all their might.

Scotty stared up toward the place where he had found the radio. Their stranger didn't seem to intend to hurt them at all. Of course, that laughter was weird enough, but—

Susan got the food supplies packed together and left them in a pile. Then she critically surveyed the boys' work. They packed everything into the jeep except the skillet. They might still be here for lunch.

After the work was finished, there was nothing to do but roam around the valley. Soon tiring of this, they walked up over the rim and through the rabbit brush and catclaw.

There was no aim or direction in their walk. But the air was fresh and clean and there were wild animals in abundance to watch. Rabbits were coming forth to meet the day and find food to take back to their young in the burrows. Gophers were scampering everywhere, waving their tiny bushy tails and chasing to the tender branches of a greasewood bush to rock to and fro in the little breeze. A half dozen deer were still wandering about from their moonlight feasting the night before. Upon arrival of the young people, however, they darted away on silent hoofs, antlered heads proud and high, eyes alert and frightened.

"We've never been in this canyon," Scotty mentioned. "Hey, look, it's a box canyon. We'd better climb up out of it before those cliffs shut us in."

Danny laughed. "You sound scared! That Indian's got you bugged, Scot!"

At which remark, Scotty grabbed Danny's ankle just ahead of and above him and gave it a yank that sent Danny sprawling. "Take that back!"

Susan gave them a look that said she'd never understand why boys had to scuffle and rassle all the time. A minute later, however, she came rushing back to them with a wild cry.

"What's the matter?" Scotty was on his feet in a second. "What did you see?"

Susan pointed, her right arm in front of her face as in self-defense. "A gila monster!"

Scotty stepped forward to take a look. "How 'bout that? A big one too. And listen to that awful hissing." He looked around. "We'll have to try this game trail over here. That gila monster sounds like that trail is all his."

They began winding their way upward, not realizing how high they were or how far they had come, until they reached a little mesa. There they paused, out of breath and wishing for a drink. When they looked back down, they were amazed and almost frightened.

Danny gasped. "And we couldn't get back down there, no matter what. That trail was steep!"

Scotty gently bit the inside of his lip. "Yeah, but the question is—Where in the world are we?"

"That shouldn't be too hard," Susan said, trembling. "If we can spot that towering mass of rocks where the Apache is, then we can find our way back to the valley."

"That's true," her brother agreed.

So they stood and searched about them in a complete circle. The crags of rock were not visible anywhere.

"But they have to—" Scotty broke off, mouth still open. "Unless—*we're on the crags!*"

"We can't be!" Danny exploded. "We didn't come that way. Nothing was familiar to us. Nothing is familiar now."

Susan stared from the great distances below, canyon after canyon, back to Scotty's face. Her eyes were wide and blue as the sky. "Could we have come—you know—that—that game trail. Some animals—like those whitetail deer—come awfully high to bed down. Maybe we are where that Apache hangs out—and we just came here another way."

They didn't want to admit it, but they were forced to. Surely there was no other answer.

"I don't see anything that looks like the place he stays," Scotty said, still not wanting to believe they had come so far.

"Your folks will be back, wanting to leave the valley," Danny said through closed teeth.

Before anyone could answer, Scotty suddenly detected a thin trail of smoke coming from behind some rocks near them. Pressing a finger to his lips, he pointed with his other hand to the spot.

"There's the Apache!"

Susan sucked in her breath. Danny hunched down

behind some yucca cactus and tried to peer through the blades of it.

Scotty set his jaw and sneaked forward a few steps. Waving a hand, he motioned for the others to follow him. Suddenly he paused and his eyes popped.

Look. He mouthed the word.

There before them, in the grassy bed among those boulders, sat a boy of perhaps seventeen. He was hunched against a rock. His body was so thin that he looked emaciated. His hair hung in long filthy strands about his face, and he was holding a thin brown cigarette between fingers that were crusted with dirt.

The eyes of the youth were nearly a red-brown, like his hair. About his shoulders was a tattered shirt, and lying on a rock beside him was the dirty poncho. He wore jeans and flimsy sandals. Scotty found it difficult to decide which were blacker—the sandals or his feet. The boy's ankles, unprotected by socks, bore many cuts and scratches.

The look in his eyes was dreamy, trancelike. He blew smoke into the air again, smiled at some inner satisfaction. "Bug out, kids," he said suddenly, quietly.

The trio stared at one another in unbelief. Questions tumbled through their minds. They stood, frozen and immovable.

"You wonder how I knew you were there?" He looked directly toward the spot where they stood. "Because my mind is sharper than all of yours put together. I'm ten feet tall, don't you know? And there's nothing I can't do! Now bug out before I do something that would hurt you."

Scotty kept staring. Once he shook his head as though unable to comprehend. It was coming clearer all the time. Not Jakob Van Loon. Not an Apache! But a hippie! *A hippie was haunting the Superstitions!*

7

THE ACID CREEP

SCOTTY HAD AN OVERWHELMING DESIRE to laugh. A hippie! And they'd tossed the idea from a coyote to a prospector to an Apache Indian. No wonder he'd stolen food. No wonder he'd taken the radio to play rock and roll. No wonder he had the poncho. Why, that was just typical hippie garb. And, as thin as his shirt was, he must have been mighty glad they brought the poncho back to him!

But—And here Scotty sobered completely. What was a hippie doing away up here? Alone. How did he get here? And how had he managed to exist until they had come along?

Susan and Danny were poised for a quick departure, but Scotty felt at ease now. Why, he and Danny had encountered kids like this at school over and over—until they were kicked out for refusing to cut their hair. Hippies were nothing new to Scotty— nor to Susan, either, for that matter. Mostly, they hadn't been dangerous. They were looking for freedom and they were rebellious. *And* they were acid users. Lysergic acid. LSD! It was the drug itself that brought these people together and caused them to form groups—colonies—where they lived, ate and slept together.

"Told you to bug out. Flake off. Scram. Don't you understand anything?"

Scotty stepped bodly into the open. "What are you doing here? Maybe—maybe we can help you."

The older youth rubbed out the stub of brown cigarette. The look in his eyes said he was still plenty high. "Help me?" A look of scorn was stamped on the sallow face. "I don't need your help, kid." A kind of smile twisted the boy's mouth. "Maybe I can help you. You look tired." He pushed a brown cigarette at Scotty so quickly that the dark-haired boy nearly lost his balance in getting out of its way.

"I don't smoke! And I sure don't want your marijuana!" Scotty felt a measure of relief when Danny drew near, with Susan right behind. "I know what it does to kids. I've seen them after school, sitting in little groups and everything gets so important to them and they go wild with some crazy kind of excitement."

The other boy was sitting on a rock and had kicked off his sandals. The smile was still there. "Sure! Life is important when you're on drugs. And when you're comin' in from a trip, you need marijuana more than ever. It brings you in nice and easy. You don't hit so hard."

Scotty felt sorry for the youth. "Aren't you afraid? I knew a kid from my class who was allowed to make his own acid in his own living room. He got an overdose and scrambled his brains. You know where Dave is now? At Twenty-fourth and Van Buren—in Phoenix!"

The long, dirty hair blew about the hippie's face.

"What's Twenty-fourth and Van Buren?" There wasn't much enthusiasm to know what occupied that address.

"It's the State Mental Hospital," Scotty frowned. "They don't think Dave will ever be right again."

"Then he didn't find on the trips what I've found. Don't you know, kid, that acid users have various reasons for taking it?"

"Like what?" Danny asked boldly, having been silent up till now.

"Like a guy that's a coward. Under LSD, he's brave. Nothing scares him. He stands taller than the world. How could anything hurt him?" The boy grinned; his teeth were jacketed over many times from not having been brushed. There wasn't one thing about him that was appealing or likable. "Or someone who wants security. There's security with other users, being a part of them. They take a trip on the acid and the world belongs to them. Everyone loves them and they love everyone. You kooks just don't have it."

"What's your name?" Susan ventured.

He looked up at her. "Pete. Now come on, you guys, get out of here!"

Scotty measured his words carefully. "We're really pulling out. You see, someone has been stealing our food and—other things. We're leaving the Superstitions around noon." He cocked his head to one side. "Say, Pete, what are you going to do for food after we're gone?"

For a moment Pete was startled out of his exhilaration. "Well, I'll be leaving the mountain too. Anyhow, I only came here the day before you did."

"Why did you?" Susan asked wonderingly. "Why

would anyone in his right m— That is, why would anyone want to come to a lonely place like this without food or water?"

Pete lifted his copper eyes, still marked with the look of an untamed animal. "I'm not a kook! You think I came here on my own?"

Danny was frowning, trying desperately to understand. "Someone brought you here? And—*left* you?"

"Hey, look at this kid! What innocence! I'm an acid creep. Don't you know that LSD—yeah, and grass too—are against the law?" He looked very smug. "And I've got both! Lots of it. Only thing is—" And there was a sudden look of sadness. "It's better where you don't use it alone. At least, it's better not to leave on a trip without someone. And it's better coming down if you know someone is there."

"And you've been using this stuff alone?"

"Was the law after you?"

"Why don't you all go away?" His eyes grew dreamy. "Sure tell you know nothing about blowing grass."

"You mean—smoking marijuana?"

"Marijuana, grass, pot—who cares? If you've never had it, you don't know what you've missed." And the dreamy look was back in his eyes and he appeared very relaxed. "For instance, you kids are putting me through the third degree. Don't you realize I don't want to talk yet?"

Scotty found himself downright curious. He had been shocked at first, then deeply troubled. Now he was terribly curious. Not about drugs. About Pete himself.

"Why do you—blow grass—after you've had

LSD?" Danny asked, stumbling over the unaccustomed term used by hippies.

"LSD brings you in hard. All of a sudden, like, you're back in this world. You get nervous, man, real nervous and tense. Grass just evens you out and brings you down easy. Acts like a sedative."

Susan shook her head as though trying to clear her mind. Her blue eyes were wide with confusion. "You can't really *like* this kind of life!"

Pete stared at her without really seeing her. Without caring. "This is out, I tell you, way out." He smiled his strange smile again. "Next time I take a trip I'm going far out—farther than ever before."

"Why?" Scotty had felt the breathless explosion rising inside of him, yet when it burst out he was surprised. "Why would a guy want to live like a filthy wild animal? There's no sense to it!"

Pete looked at Scotty and saw him. "I told you, guys take acid for many reasons—mostly to solve problems. But me—and others—take it because—because we found something out there on the trips." He shook his shaggy head, and parts of his hair were so matted with dirt that the strands didn't even separate. "You're straight people. That's why I'd never tell you. You see, you have to know something about God before you'd ever understand."

Scotty's mouth dropped open but he couldn't make a sound. He shook his head, doubting his own senses at this point. Then he dropped to one knee near Pete. "What do you mean?"

"Just what I said. A guy would have to know about God and—and *want* Him—before he could understand why I take LSD."

"We know God!" Susan cried passionately.

Pete's strange red-brown eyes lifted toward the girl. "You puttin' me on?"

"We all know God," Danny said earnestly. "We received Jesus into our lives a long time ago. We belong to Him! He's our Saviour!"

Pete did not speak for a long time. He fixed his gaze upon the grass, finally plucked a stem and stuck it in his mouth. "I don't dig you, man. About a Saviour, I mean. I just understand God and I found Him out there. The farther out I go, the more I find Him."

"You—" Scotty felt sick inside. And perplexed. "You find God out—on the—trips?"

"That's right. On the trips. All my life I looked for God, but no one ever told me how to find Him. I went to a couple of churches even, but I couldn't feel Him there. Out there," he emphasized, "I met Him. First trip. His presence comes near to me and we walk and talk together." He sighed dreamily. "No one ever told me I could find Him through LSD."

Susan opened her mouth, but Scotty motioned for her not to speak. No one spoke; but each one was praying. Praying for Pete. Praying for some kind of an answer.

"What—what is it like?" Scotty asked finally.

"I guess it's like heaven. He comes to me and I feel Him near. I see Him in the trees, I hear Him in the waterfall down below; I find Him in the mountains. He's everywhere. He's in everything. Don't you see?" He held out his arms to them. "I can never give Him up!"

"Pete!" It was a cry to the hippie's very heart.

It held Scotty's frustration and unbelief in reaction to
what he had just heard. "Pete, it's not that way! You
don't find God through drugs. Oh, Pete, listen to
me now. If you really met God out—out *there*—He
would witness to you of His Son, Jesus Christ. There's
no salvation without Jesus, Pete. You have to believe
in your heart that Jesus died on the cross for your
sins and that only His blood can wash your sins
away—"

Pete shook his head firmly, and his lips were
pressed together in disapproval. "I have found God.
I don't know about anything else. I don't know about
Jesus—just His name. No one ever told me. You see,
Scotty—the rest of you—" He gestured. "It's easy for
you to tell me that I haven't found God. But you've
never been with me on my trips. I have been there
with Him. I know."

Scotty pulled his New Testament from his shirt
pocket. Something within him said that he was going
too far, trying to cram too much at Pete. On the
other hand, this could be his only chance to tell Pete
about Jesus. He must plant the seed of the Word
while there was opportunity.

How could Pete feel the presence of God while
stoned on LSD?

"Look, Pete, read it for yourself. Try to understand. This is God's Word, His letter to the world.
Read it, Pete!"

*"Neither is there salvation in any other: for there
is none other name under heaven given among men,
whereby we must be saved."*

Pete read it silently, his red-brown hair hanging
in dirty, matted strings about his swarthy face. "I

don't understand this," he pointed out quickly. "But I *do* understand what I've found out there. Don't you see? It's God I want—the reality of God! This—" He handed the New Testament back to Scotty with a slightly curled lip. "I don't dig this."

"Pete!" Scotty scooted nearer. He never dreamed a human being could smell so terrible. "I believe that what you've found seems real to you; but God can never be real unless you know Jesus. He's God's Son and He died for your sins." He wished he had the words! "Pete, you need someone to help you."

"I don't need any help." Pete leaned back with his eyes closed. So far as he was concerned the conversation ended.

"You said you'd be leaving the mountain," Scotty persisted. "Why don't you come down to the valley with us? We can give you a ride down off the mountain."

A slow smile curved Pete's lips. "Me? You're kiddin'. Look at me real good. Your parents are straight people. I'm an acid head. They wouldn't want to take me anywhere."

8

THE ROCKSLIDE

SUSAN HAD A HARD TIME to keep from laughing. It was a sure thing that her parents were "straight"! She could hardly imagine them as hippies. "But they *will* take you down the mountain," she encouraged. "Our parents are kind, and they care. They'll care about you."

Pete shook his head stubbornly. "I've got sugar cubes. I've got acid to make them as strong as I want. I have marijuana. Besides all that, I've been chased by the police once. Your folks find that out, they'll dump me at the nearest police station. Just the way," he continued bitterly, "my friends dumped me off at the foot of these mountains when we were being chased."

"Is that how you got here?" Danny asked.

"You kids make me sick! You don't know anything." He paused, working his dirty feet back into the sandals. "Sure. I was high—real far out on the acid. Usually you can act sober and make sense when you talk. But I couldn't. I was driving and—the lights began to change. Changing and changing and overlapping in their colors. The stop and go lights were brilliant and stunning. One minute the street was a thousand miles wide, and the next it was a narrow little street where you could barely squeeze in to meet another car. I wasn't sure of anything.

"The were three others with me, two girls and another kid about seventeen. They begged to take over the driving, but I wouldn't let them. The wind hit my face and the colors turned into prisms of light and color that thrilled me! Then the siren came. I guess I was doing about sixty-five there on East Van Buren.

"I knew I'd never be able to fake it out, so I stepped on the gas and we did some traveling. We hit a hundred and five once close to Apache Junction. Then I found an old road leading toward the Superstitions, and I still thought I could lose the cop following us.

"My friends were frantic. They're hippies, but they weren't high—I had all the stuff." He stopped, remembering with a frown what had happened. "I had to slow down to make a sharp curve and it was a dirt road; and next thing I was being shoved out of the car and they went on without me."

"What happened after that?"

"I rolled down a hill and into a clump of catclaw. The siren tore by and I heard both cars stop down the road about a half mile."

"And you came here to hide?"

"Not exactly. I did make a wild scramble into the hills to make sure the cop didn't find me, but, being as far out as I was, I didn't know I came so far or so high. The hallucinations had begun and, in the moonlight, the canyons were all filled with silver bushes and bright yellow rocks. I seemed to soar

with the wind. It was wonderful and it must have
lasted quite a few hours."

"And you weren't afraid?" Susan asked.

"Afraid?" the youth repeated, surprised. "How can
you be afraid when the presence of God is so near?
He walked with me, and I found him everywhere.
He—he filled everything! The trees, the little valley
where the waterfall laughed and sparkled like millions
of colorful drops and streams."

The trio listened, confused and amazed. At times
Pete spoke like a poet. At other times he was more
like a rebel from skid row.

"Pete? Pete, you're just plain *you* now. Please believe me. Unless this presence you tell us about speaks
to you of Jesus Christ, it's all wrong. You can't know
God until you know Him through Christ."

Nothing could shake Pete's confidence. "I know
Him," he said simply.

How? *How?* HOW? Scotty would not have admitted it for worlds, but it was bothering him dread-
fully. How could a hippie take LSD and then feel
God's presence and be made so joyous as a result?
The whole business was confusing, shocking! It bugged him. And, from the looks upon the faces of his
sister and his friend, they too were going through
the same thing. Yet there was an answer somewhere.
Scotty wished he knew what it was.

"What do you feel now?" Danny dared to ask.

Pete looked at the sky. Then he rubbed his nose
against the ragged shirt sleeve. "Now? I feel OK. A
little depressed maybe." He smiled sheepishly. "I
guess—maybe—I'm even glad you came along. But
everything's drab now. No color. No brightness. Back

from a world that's bright and thrilling to—*this*. You see, I know what I must look like and—how I must smell. But I don't care. I don't want to do anything about it. I guess there's really just a desire, a waiting, till I can take another sugar cube."

"They say that— Well, don't you ever get the feeling that—that your mind is being affected?" Scotty paused and pulled in his lower lip. "That it might crumble?"

"I've had it that way. Especially when you come in without a sedative. You can hit too hard."

"Come with us," Scotty implored. "You have to leave the mountain anyway. You can't stay without food. Of course," he added slowly, "you do have a piece of ham, but it'll spoil here in the sunlight and you'll be poisoned when you eat it. Then what?"

Scotty thought he had scored a point there, so he continued doggedly. "And you don't dare take LSD again without anyone being here with you. You're using too much, even for a hippie."

"My mind is strong," Pete protested.

"Dave's was too," Danny said quietly.

Pete hesitated. "Well— I can't be here without food. Not that you want much when you're on acid, but—"

Scotty suddenly remembered something he had been told by a teacher in school that past year. A hippie had cut his hair and entered school but had been unable to concentrate on his studies and soon dropped out. His teacher had said, "Hippies on acid find it impossible to concentrate on studies to get passing grades. Another of their difficulties is making decisions. Their muscles don't get flabby, but their will does. They can't seem to make up their minds."

All right then, Scotty was going to try and make Pete's mind up for him. It might not work, but he'd give it a try.

"Grab your poncho, Pete, and let's go." He looked at his watch. "A quarter till two! And Dad wanted to leave early!" Real concern gripped him now. "Hurry, Pete!"

Scotty took Pete's poncho himself and stuck the smelly thing under his arm. Maybe he could even trick Pete into taking a bath!

Suddenly Pete seemed anxious, almost brooding. Nervous. He dug into some brush in back of a rock and pulled out a small brown bag, which he tied to his belt. Then he pulled his poncho out from under Scotty's arm and slipped it over his head, thus completely concealing the bag.

It came to Scotty sharply that they might be guilty of disregarding the law and being a party to the concealment of drugs.

Susan heard her name being called while yet some distance from the valley. She lifted her face, cupped her mouth and called back; but the wind caught the sound and sent it into fragments. She called again.

"I think they heard me, Scot. But they're probably wondering if the earth swallowed us."

Now that Pete had resigned himself to come, he seemed more or less happy about the whole thing. But Scotty couldn't help wondering what his father's reaction was going to be. And his mother's! Of course, they would both hide their feelings and never let Pete be hurt.

They dipped into the last small canyon and up the other side, stepping over the rim and into the lovely green valley. After being in the hot brown hills all day, it looked better than ever. Sparkling waterfall forming the stream below. Blowing and dashing droplets like millions of dazzling jewels. The golden sand and great, towering cottonwoods. The great boulders and deep, thick grass. Would Pete like it too? Oh, but then, he'd been there several times already!

The hippie removed his sandals and waded in luxury through the grass. "Feels good to sore feet," he said.

"Go dip them in the water," Danny suggested. "That should be even better."

Up to your neck, Scotty thought, smiling inwardly.

"Scot! Susan! All of you, where—" Mr. Hanson got no further. His lips were still parted, but he stopped cold.

Scotty pointed a thumb toward Pete. "This is our haunt," he said quickly. "Our hungry haunt who likes rock and roll. His name is Pete. Pete, this is my father, Mr. Hanson. And my mother, Mrs. Hanson."

The tall man stooped a little, making him seem shorter. "Well, come over by the stream and—and we'll talk. There has to be a story behind this one."

Mrs. Hanson was frying rabbit—they'd shot five that morning—and she stood watching the others head for the stream as though not quite believing what she saw. Taking another look to be certain all the meat was done, she turned off the fire and marched along behind them. This was one time she was going to hear firsthand.

When she really got a good look at Pete, however,

it was no longer in simple curiosity. Compassion poured through her heart for the youth. Who was he and how had he ever gotten into such a terrible condition?

The story was rehearsed again, and the parents heard it all exactly as it had happened. They sat in perfect silence, however, after it was over.

It was Mrs. Hanson who made the first move. "Well! I have meat in the skillet and plenty of it. I even baked some potatoes, so we have quite a feast here in the wilds. Pete, you will join us, of course. But I know you'll want to bathe first; it's been such a long time. So Susan and I will just take a stroll. But hurry, because we're all starved."

Pete's mouth dropped open and he blinked at Scotty's mother several times. *A bath?* That was for straight people! But after a moment he closed his lips and nodded. "A bath? Sure. Sure. A—bath."

Scotty got him a clean pair of jeans, for there wasn't too much difference in their height. Otherwise Pete donned the same dirty sandals and poncho. But he looked so much better the fellows could hardly believe it. They'd even managed not to laugh when Pete had stepped into the icy stream. The water had run brown for a few minutes, but finally the matting was gone from his hair and his face was scrubbed fairly well. Danny took it upon himself to take the washcloth and rub the dirt ring in front of his ears until it disappeared.

"You really look pretty good," Mr. Hanson commented, grinning. "Call your mother and Susan, Scot, and we'll eat."

Pete put a hand on his stomach. " 'Sfunny. I really do feel hungry."

He was almost good-looking when he grinned. "And I have to admit that it's good to be with people again. Without being afraid they'd find me stealing something!"

They laughed about that. "You know," Mr. Hanson announced, "we may even stay overnight and leave first thing in the morning. There's no Apache to fear and I imagine Pete could use a good night's sleep before going home."

Scotty squared his shoulders. Pride for his father welled up inside his heart. Why, he was including Pete—not like he was a dirty, long-haired hippie, but as a human being. Love. That's what it was. And it could get to a person quicker than anything in the world.

"A home—" Pete said, holding out his paper plate for the meat and baked potato. "I'm not sure just what a home is. My mother sits in a saloon all day instead of keeping house or getting meals. My dad— well, dad's OK, really, but I've never seen much of him. He's working all the time and gone so much. If that's what a home is, then I suppose I do have one."

For a few minutes the rabbit and baked potatoes were forgotten. All lifted thoughtful eyes to one another. Their faces were troubled. Their hearts went out to this strange boy. If they had had a homelife like that, maybe they'd have been hippies too.

Then Mrs. Hanson took the situation into her own hands. With a laugh she said, "Susan, if you don't get your plate a little closer, this meat will be cold before you eat it!"

It was a quarter to five. Already the sun was low and there was the feeling of chill in the air.

When they were through eating, the boys carried the sleeping bags back into the valley, leaving the jeep where it sat, just over the rim of the valley on the slope of a canyon. Then they brought enough food for breakfast.

Night seemed to come faster than usual that night, but no one was in a hurry to go to bed. They sat on the sand by the water and discussed again the problems involved in taking LSD. The bad trips. The freak-outs, when one lost all sense of being in one's body, and lost besides the knowledge of where and who he was.

To Scotty and Susan and Danny, the terms meant very little. But that the acid was something to fear as much as one would fear drinking a glass of poison was certain in their minds.

"Aren't you ever afraid of crashing too hard?" Mr. Hanson asked Pete. "Of ruining your mind completely? I've heard of hippies who take an overdose, and their minds are so affected that they're never the same again."

Pete picked up a stick and began tracing in the sand. "I don't dig you people." There was a trace of sadness in the youth's voice. "You all say you're Christians. Yet, when I tell you about finding God through LSD, you won't believe me. How is it that you say you know God and yet you don't want His presence?"

"Pete, son, you've got it all wrong. God can't be

put in a drug or a test tube. You can't find Him on your trips any more than you can find Him behind the counter in a drugstore."

The sadness in Pete's eyes was real. He bowed his head and said nothing.

There was an awful, nagging misery in Scotty's heart. He wanted to be alone, wanted to think. If what Pete found wasn't the presence of God, then what was it? That was what he wanted to know.

Pete stayed close in for night devotions. Mr. Hanson gave the Bible to Danny that night for Scripture reading. And Danny took some time, all grim and serious, to think about it. When he opened the Bible, it was to the book of John. He read from the third chapter, his voice trembling but determined. When he came to verse 16, Scotty realized how much his friend cared what happened to Pete:

" 'For God so loved the world that he gave his only begotten Son, that whosoever believeth in him should not perish but have everlasting life. For God sent not his Son into the world to condemn. . . .' "

What was it? What was it Pete found out there that he thought was God? What was the answer? That had been one of the greatest jolts Scotty had ever experienced. But there was peace in his heart again now. For whatever—whoever—Pete encountered, it certainly was not God.

Pete was lying beside Scotty. The hippie had been given a clean shirt and Mr. Hanson had pulled a heavy wool blanket from the jeep for him. The poncho had been laid aside for the night and Pete was quite acceptable—so far as smell was concerned.

"This is sure better than sleeping on the cold grass over there last night," Pete murmured, yawning.

Scotty lifted his head and looked toward the other boy. "What do you mean—'over there'?"

"Over there. Thirty yards from here, I suppose. It was so lonely up there I couldn't stand it. I crept into the valley after I thought you were all asleep, then left just before it began to get light."

"But—" Scotty lowered his voice to just above a whisper. "The laughter! We heard you up there laughing!"

Pete stuck his thumb in his chest. "You didn't hear *me,* man! Because I heard it too, and I'm here to let you know I was more than glad to be near other people."

"But—if you didn't laugh—*who did?*"

"I don't know!"

"Don't say anything to the others," Scotty urged. "Everyone would get all stirred up and it wouldn't do any good. Anyhow, we'll be pulling out in the mor—"

"What's that?"

Scotty sat up, tense and alarmed. "It's—I don't know, but it's wild!"

There was a faraway rumble, high on the ridge above them. Then suddenly it was coming closer. Closer! In the moonlight a great cloud of mist or dust was streaming down the mountainside!

"Dad! Mom! Wake up!"

Mr. Hanson struggled from his sleeping bag. Susan and Mrs. Hanson unzipped their bags and sat up. Danny was fighting to wake up.

The rumble had changed into a roar that was coming closer and closer every second! Even in the moonlight it was hard to say exactly what was happening.

"A rockslide, everyone!" It was Scotty's father who shouted the terrifying words. "We've got to get out of here fast! Hurry! *Hurry!*"

9

PETE

WITH THOSE WORDS, every person in camp tore out of their sleeping bags. Pete threw off his blanket, tripped and fell. A small bag tied to his belt was ripped off and he stared wildly in the moonlight, stooped and sought to retrieve the drugs.

Scotty caught his shoulder and pulled. "Come on, leave it, Pete! You'll be killed!"

Leaving everything behind—bedrolls, food, water and other supplies—they made a dash from the valley. Falling, scrambling, helping one another, they at last threw themselves into a canyon and crouched behind a heap of great boulders.

The rockslide had appeared to have a slow start, but it quickly gathered momentum as it roared down toward the valley. It looked as if the entire mountainside were cascading toward the spot where they had been seconds before. Great rocks broke forth from the rockslide, bouncing and tumbling into the valley. Occasionally a boulder would come tumbling near them. For the most part, however, the slide was shifting—and shifting yet more. Boulders as big as Cadillacs crashed on the other side of the valley. Tons of rocks and dirt came sliding down, then heaped up to form another small mountain.

Clouds of dust rose to dizzying heights, covering canyons for miles around.

It was a long time before Mr. Hanson ventured from their hiding place; for now and again another big rock would come crashing down. He took off his hat and struck it against his leg to shake off the dust. Then he climbed to the rim of the valley, only to take a step backward in amazement.

"Let me go first," he called back. He'd grabbed his powerful flashlight from beside his sleeping bag when he'd run, and now he shone its beam ahead of him. He surveyed the boulder-strewn valley, which was scarcely recognizable because of the added rocks and dirt. Finally, when he was really certain the slide was over, he returned to his family.

"You can come back," he said soberly. "Come here, I want to show you where we were sleeping."

They made their way toward the stream. Mr. Hanson stopped and pointed to a mass of torn and shredded cloth upon which lay a boulder the size of their jeep. "If you hadn't been awake and heard the first of the slide," Mr. Hanson said, "that's where we'd be."

Scotty stared and his head felt light. "You mean—that's where we were sleeping?"

Mrs. Hanson clung to her husband's arm with both hands. The full impact of what had happened was just beginning to hit them all.

"We ought to fall down and thank the Lord that we're still alive!" Susan whispered. "Oh, how awful!"

Suddenly Mr. Hanson stiffened. He glanced toward the other side of the valley. "I was too concerned about everyone before, but—I think we've lost the jeep."

"The jeep!" Danny yelled.

"What'll we do now, Dad?" Scotty asked.

His father attempted a grin. "We'll never come here again, that's what."

Walking to the crest of the hill leading to the other side of the canyon, the group stared in dismay. A massive hill stood where the jeep had been. It was covered with tons of dirt and rocks and was no doubt hopelessly crushed. Even the rugged trail leading to the valley was erased for a long way.

While they stood there, a rock loosened from the hillside and came rumbling down the mountain to rest silently against the great mass already collected.

"Mr. Hanson?" This was Pete, whose thin frame was trembling visibly and whose sunken eyes expressed sheer terror. "Your—your jeep's gone. The sleeping bags. Maybe even the food. How are you going to get down? It'll take too long for your wife and Susan. They'd never make it. And—doesn't all this loss worry you?"

"I'm too thankful for all of us to be alive and unhurt, Pete. Aren't you glad for that?"

Pete thought for a minute. "I guess so."

Mr. Hanson led the way back to the valley. His hand was on Pete's shoulder. "Did you take a—a loss too, Pete?"

The youth shrugged. "Sure!" he replied readily. "But I know where I can get more." He didn't pull away from the man's hand. Rather, he regarded him with respect. "Do you know where you can get another jeep?"

"In time, the Lord willing." Mr. Hanson and Pete paused beside the stream, thankful that the waterfall was undamaged and that the stream still flowed along undisturbed. "But, Pete, why would you want to get more of the drug? Don't you realize—"

Now Pete did pull away. "I realize that the same God you say saved us tonight walks with me on a trip—and He'll never let anything hurt me either!" With this, Pete walked barefoot to the boulder that had landed on their sleeping bags and sat down.

They didn't realize until morning that every person in the group had lost their shoes, and that actually they were stranded in this place. It could take many long, hot days to make it down the mountain. "Well," Danny said softly to his friend, "it may have been Pete who stole things from us, but he sure didn't cause that rockslide tonight!"

"It wasn't him who laughed that night either," Scotty replied. "No, the laughter has happened before. So have the rockslides! Crashing down in the dead of night and killing campers before they could escape."

Pete was definitely a loner the day after the slide. He sat on the boulder that had shredded their sleeping bags and brooded. Several times he stuck one hand into his pocket, fingered an object and withdrew his hand again.

All the food they had left was the oleo and canned milk in their little cache by the stream, nearly a full box of pancake mix, a box of cornmeal and two potatoes. The bottle of maple syrup had been smashed the night before and lay in the dirt with ants swarming over the sticky mess. The camp stove and cooking utensils had been spared miraculously.

"How can we get along without our shoes, Dad?" Scotty asked, coming to stand beside his father.

"My boots are drying out," his father answered. "I found them floating in the water this morning. But all the others have disappeared. And the extra shoes were in the jeep. I've got to do some planning this morning—figure out a way to get down this mountain without shoes, water and food." The grim look on his face said it was a problem not easy to solve.

"We can always carry a supply of water in your boots," Scotty said, not trying to be funny.

"That's true enough. Seems like all we've been doing since we got here is to try and get away again."

"Won't it be easy to follow the road down?"

"In a lot of places the road has disappeared entirely."

Scotty tried to put himself in his father's position. He'd have to get them down the quickest way because of all existing conditions. Running into cliffs hundreds of feet high—canyons with no way out except the same way they entered. Without the jeep and their prized compass, it was going to be a hard and dangerous trip.

Pete was no help. He'd made it up the mountain under the influence of a powerful drug. He'd bragged he could get down, but today he admitted that he had no idea of the way to go.

"Maybe we ought to stay right here and try to signal a passing plane," Scotty suggested. "Mom's shredding potatoes into the pancake batter to make them go further. Then she's got the makings for fried cornmeal cakes. I know it's not the best food in the world, but it will keep us alive, if we can send up some kind of a distress signal."

Mr. Hanson propped a bare foot against a rock.

"Now look, son, someone is out to get us. That's obvious to everyone in camp. Tonight they might succeed—if we stay here. Then there's Pete." He paused to moisten his lips and glance toward the hippie, dreamily staring into space from his perch. "Who knows whether he might take LSD again, and what wild things he might come up with if he did."

"His bag that he kept the drugs in was ripped off his belt last night in his hurry to escape the rockslide. I think he lost it all." Scotty turned and pointed. "It was right about there, and all that's there now is about a ton of rocks."

Mr. Hanson's eyes narrowed thoughtfully. "I believe he has a sugar cube with acid on it in his pocket, Scot. At least he's got something in there that he doesn't want to lose. See, he can't keep his hand off it."

"Surely he wouldn't goof things up now, Dad."

His father shook his head slowly. "Let's hope not. We haven't got time to go chasing through the hills after a hippie!" He was smiling, but underneath there was a sober heart.

The group was glad enough for potato pancakes with oleo, minus syrup. There was coffee too, and even the younger ones drank it this morning.

Pete halfheartedly pushed a few bites of food down. He was off somewhere. He wasn't with them. After a little while he wandered off to the place where he had sat before, and then again he watched both sky and water. Instinctively Scotty knew that Pete was remembering "God" being in the water, the trees, everything! So Pete had declared yesterday.

Scotty looked up again, just in time to see Pete slip

something from his pocket. He held it for a moment between thumb and forefinger. Slowly, and with a dreamy look, he opened his mouth and placed the sugar cube on his tongue. Twenty minutes from now he'd be in heaven.

Scotty dashed from the group, plunged toward Pete in a desperate move to get the sugar cube from him. But he knew in his heart it was too late.

"Pete! Pete, why'd you do it? You're crazy! Why did you do it?"

Pete's copper eyes were sad. "You say you know God!" the youth responded in an angry whisper, holding Scotty at arm's length. "Your father even spoke to Him before we ate breakfast. But you don't want me to have Him! I can't understand that!"

Scotty's low voice was filled with anguish. "It's not God you're meeting, Pete. It's a—a spirit. A demon spirit or something, but it's not God!"

Pete was wearing an old watch that left green marks on his arm. He looked at it and smiled. He wanted to get away, to walk high into the mountains and into the presence of God. Something about that thrilled his soul and opened to him new visions and hallucinations of paradise.

"Twenty minutes," Pete murmured softly, and leaned back in the sunshine.

The others were still eating and had not interfered, hoping that Scotty could handle the problem. When he came back alone, however, Mr. Hanson set his cup of coffee aside. He had not seen Pete take the sugar cube, but he'd sensed all morning that the youth would take acid, if he'd managed to save any.

Scotty sat down on his rock "stool" and looked at

the pancake on his plate. It made him feel sick and he decided to eat it later. They dared not throw away a scrap of food at this point.

His father jerked his head toward the stream. "What's up?"

"Pete managed to salvage one sugar cube last night," Scotty said, not looking directly at anyone in particular. "He took it."

Mr. Hanson looked tired. "I should never have allowed him to wander over there alone, but—he's not mine to order around." He groaned. "I was wrong on that score!"

"Dad, don't you think we ought to bring him over here and not let him get out of our—"

"You're too late, Scot. He's gone."

10

WHERE ARE YOU, GOD?

A SENSE OF UNEASINESS fell over the group. Their eyes quickly scanned the whole valley, but it was no use. Pete was gone. And with him had gone the transistor radio which had been somehow saved the night before.

Mr. Hanson snapped into action. "He can't have gone far. The only way he could have left the valley since the slide last night was past the place where we took shelter. Let's spread out a little and comb that canyon. He couldn't have gone any farther than that."

"Right!" Danny agreed and the others murmured agreement too.

It was easy to run in their bare feet through the grassy floor of the valley; but once they rose over the rim and stepped down onto the rough, rocky soil of the canyon, the going became more and more difficult.

While Susan spent most of her time ouch-ing over burs in her feet, Scotty leaped skillfully from rock to rock. He exclaimed at last, "He's not in here, Dad! Danny and I will run up the game trail and see if he's on his way back to his 'high place.'"

Danny was right behind him. "What do you mean, 'high place'?"

Scotty glanced back unsmiling. "I shouldn't have said that, Danny. A high place in the Bible was where people used to worship other gods."

"Well, that's what Pete's doing all right."

"You know what, Danny?" Scotty caught a rocky ledge and pulled himself up. "Pete doesn't have any marijuana with him to use as a sedative when he comes down."

"You're sure about that?" Danny caught up with his friend. There was no sign of Pete around. "That means he could really crash-land when this trip is over, unless—unless there's someone with him."

"That's right." Scotty paused, looking back the way they had come. But there was no sound, no sign of movement. "How did he disappear so fast?"

"Well, I sure—Hey, Scot, take a look at this! Over here on this rock. Isn't that blood?"

Scotty reached down with a finger and touched the red sticky drop. "It sure is. It must be Pete. He probably cut one of his feet again. And it's fresh too!" Scotty pursed his lips in determination. "Let's go after him, Danny!"

*   *   *

Pete had perched on the boulder beside the rushing, gurgling stream that morning half in anger. Anger that no one there would believe him when he said that through LSD he had found God. With the anger, there was a great rebellion that rose up within him. He didn't need the Hansons. He'd show them. He'd managed to retrieve one sugar cube last night and no grass. He'd take the acid and stay right here and show them that he knew God!

The minutes began to pass, however, and Scotty

came and talked with him. Something was gnawing inside of him. He wanted to get away, to be alone to keep his tryst with God.

He watched Scotty return to the group. All backs were turned to him for a few moments. Pete tried to fight down the desire to leave; but it had been the same way in California. Twenty minutes after taking the acid, there always had been that drive to get away, to be alone. Pete had always slipped away from the group and headed down to the water's edge. There, with the gentle waves of the Pacific lapping over his feet, he had met God as he had launched out on his trip.

Now the desire burned within him. The drug was taking hold. Whatever he was going to do, it had to be now. So, without ever having meant to do so, Pete slipped over the edge of the rock, slid into the icy water and waded around the left side of the waterfall. He swung the last few feet over the top and was gone. Already his vision had changed so that the waterfall was a glorious cascade of silver, blue, red and yellow. He fell into a trot—a steady trot that took him higher and higher toward the craggy peaks once more. His poncho hung limply about his thin body, and his hair tumbled down over it in wild disarray. He felt tired today, depressed and anxious to keep his appointment. How had he ever thought that he could go off on a trip with straight people all around?

Higher and higher still, with the wind billowing the poncho and cooling his flesh. Laughter, sheer laughter, rose up within him, and he stood upon a frail pinnacle of rock and let it roll. Everything inside of him was becoming exhilarated. An eagerness to know the whole world took hold of him. He thrilled and wondered at the blue of the sky and the white of the thunderheads, at the glory of blue, purple, red and yellow that covered the mountainsides. What a world to live in! Wonderful world!

Ah, this was life—at its fullest, its best. He felt as tall as the sheer pinnacles that rose above him.

Then he thought himself to be at the ocean's edge. He trailed his feet leisurely through the gentle waves and was shocked to discover that they scratched and cut his feet. He saw again the tiny gems rising out of the salt spray, dazzling, glittering—and did not know that what he saw was a product of his own imagination. He was beginning to groove in his hallucinations.

The presence will come now, he thought. He must be patient. It would come, because it always had. Was it possible that today this—this Jesus would come instead of God? For the Hansons had said that Jesus was the Son of God and that one could know God only through knowing Jesus. Oh, but what a mixed-up tale!

It was the presence. The presence that Pete loved and wanted so desperately. Was that his crutch? After all, LSD was a crutch to everyone who took it. The acid was to meet some kind of failing point, some dissatisfaction in life. Pete's was loneliness, insecurity. If acid could bring him the presence of God and meet his need, then let it be a crutch.

A slithering green snake suddenly appeared at Pete's feet, and he sidestepped it with a feeling of terror. He hated snakes, had always hated them and been fearful of them.

It was amazing how far Pete had come and how

high he had climbed in so short a time. It seemed he
had taken on the feet of a deer and had bounded forward without the slightest effort.

"Why don't You come to me, God? Where are
You?"

He walked on, very slowly now. The radiant lights
and colors were less radiant now, just when they
should have grown to unlimited brilliance. Was he
going to have a bad trip? He never had!

Great clumps of greasewood appeared in front of
Pete and he began going around them carefully. He
stopped, confused. It had looked as though he could
go around them; but now that he was closer, he found
that he must walk through them instead.

A shiver passed over him. It looked so dark inside
the bushes. And the thunderheads had disappeared
too. For one stark moment Pete could not remember
where he was.

The transistor radio, banged and bumped throughout this trip, hung limply in Pete's hand. Suddenly remembering it, he flipped the dial. Light, lilting music
burst forth. It wasn't to Pete's liking. He needed
music right now that had a beat. A beat that would
match the beat of his heart and pound into the throb
of his veins, that would captivate his mind and body
so utterly that it would become a part of him. That
would surely help him if this was going to be a bad
trip.

Another snake uncurled from beneath a bush and
passed over his bare and bleeding feet. A cry escaped
the boy's lips. But before he could move, there were
other snakes. A moment before, they had appeared
on the ground as fallen twigs, but he'd been wrong.

For now they were snakes, hideous, in all shapes, lengths and colors. Some were coiled as though to strike. Others lay staring at him with cold, passive eyes, watching his every move. Others slid after him and over his ankles, and he heard a strange voice screaming and screaming—and did not know that it was his own.

"Go away!" he yelled. "Get away from me! I'm afraid! I'm afraid!"

Pete buried his ashen face in his poncho and sobbed like a tormented child. "Where are You, God? *God, where are You?*" When he opened his eyes at last, still shaking violently, he began screaming again—shrill, piercing screams that echoed and re-echoed through the mountains.

"My God! My body has been cut off! Look! I'm gone." He covered his face with trembling hands. "I'm gone from the waist down!"

Pete tried to move. Living horror dogged him. What had happened? Where was the presence that had always met him, walked with him before? Why hadn't He come? He'd never refused before.

In vain Pete explored his body, searching for the part that was missing. He sobbed in agony, tore his clothes, dug his filthy fingers into his scalp. His face, already dirty, was streaked by rivers of anguished tears. His hair was matted, stringy and wet from both tears and perspiration. He was a madman. A teenage madman roaming the Superstition Mountains, searching for the other half of his body.

And then, slowly, something began to happen to Pete that brought him a measure of relief. In his tormented mind, he took off the top half of his body and laid it among the greasewood bushes, then in some mysterious way Pete stepped away from his body and began to walk.

It seemed he walked for many long hours. Sometimes his path led through such glorious scenes that he could hardly bear it. It was like some bright, lovely dream where one stepped high and breathed in the pure perfume of delight. But the yearned-for presence did not come. He heard his voice calling, "Where are You, God? Why don't You come? God, God, where are You?"

Other times his path led through darkness. Darkness that pressed close to mind, body and spirit, where one moved among lurking shadows and terrifying faces. Where small men in ridiculous and hideous masks and clothing jeered and scoffed at him. And their presence walked with him along those fearful paths, clung to him at moments like horrible leeches, trying to enter his body. And Pete would hear his voice again, pleading, screaming, agonizing.

Wildly he began searching for the half of his body he had left behind. Even half a body was better than none at all. He scrambled into every small dip in the area, explored every clump of rocks and brush. Frantically he looked among the crags, and almost fell over the side of the mountain for his efforts.

Recovering himself from this near encounter with death, he pulled back against the safety of the ground and sobbed frantically.

There! There it was, exactly where he had left it. He ran toward it, crying brokenly. The small, ugly men were right on his heels, gaining on him every second. He pulled and tugged at the limp form in front of him. He couldn't seem to get in. Even though the lower half of his body was back with the top half, he couldn't get into it. It felt like a costume of some sort, limp but heavy; and though he struggled with it desperately, nothing seemed to work.

Panic seized him and held him captive. "I can't get back in!" He screamed it over and over. "I can't get back into my body! Help me! Please help me! Somebody help me get back into my body!"

11

A LEDGE OF PURE GOLD

THERE WAS NO STOPPING for Scotty Hanson after seeing the blood on the trail before him. With amazing speed he climbed forward, his face set and his muscles tense. Pete was there, somewhere before them, and he was going to need help. His father would never want him to turn back or give up under that circumstance.

"He must go crazy on that stuff," Danny said once, his chest heaving from the effort of keeping up with Scotty.

"You probably pegged it, all right."

Hand over hand, Scotty pulled himself up the last narrow incline. His feet were cut and scratched and fairly aching for the icy stream they had left.

"Remember when that guy Robert what's-his-face tried to sell us a sugar cube from his car after school?"

"And he was caught and tried and sent to the prison in Florence, Arizona. They found enough acid in his car to paralyze the city of Tucson, the police said!"

"Yeah." Danny missed his toehold, scrambled to correct his balance and followed on to level ground again. "And about that same time in a newspaper article, it said that LSD confuses the sight and sound reactions—so that sight impulses get jumbled into the sound department. And sound tries to become sight. Wow!"

"It's weird. Fact, when Pete called himself an acid creep, he said it right. It *is* creepy. Maybe I'm stupid, but I just don't see why teenagers want to take a chance on blowing their brains by this junk."

They walked side by side now that they had reached the summit. There was neither sight of Pete nor clue to follow at this point.

"You're not stupid," Danny said, throwing himself to the ground. He lay gasping for breath and his eyes closed for a few moments. Regaining his strength, he sat up, wrapped his arms around his knees and stared away through the maze of canyons that fell away before them. Scotty joined him.

"Did you happen to notice those clouds up there?" Scotty asked.

"I've tried not to." Danny looked at his watch. "It's one o'clock, and my stomach's bugging about that something terrible."

"The sun's under a cloud," Scotty persisted. "A dark cloud. But it does make it cooler."

Danny turned to his friend with a look of woe. "Your dad wanted to start down the mountain, Scot. We're going to be out of food, and he's not sure of the way. And we've got to think about your mother too!"

Scotty traced the path of an ant that was crawling at his feet. "I don't know what to do," he confessed. "Dad sent us out to get Pete. He wouldn't want to leave him behind—especially alone and on LSD!"

Danny gritted his teeth and tried to keep back the

words that rose to his lips. He wanted to cry out,
"Come on, Scot, let's turn back! It'll get dark if a
storm's coming, and we'll wind up lost in the Superstitions, and then there won't be any hope for us!"
But he kept his teeth clenched until he knew he had
control of himself, then he got to his feet. "Let's see
if we can find him, Scot."

And Scotty, who had understood his friend's con-
flict, acted as though that was exactly what they had
planned all along. For, if Danny had spoken the
words, Scotty was afraid he might have been willing
to give up too.

The fellows made the most of every grassy place
they walked through and trod very carefully where
there were rocks and cactus.

"You think he's really followed this trail?" Danny
did ask at last.

Scotty frowned. "I don't know. Seems like we ought
to see or find something soon." He brushed his leg
against a prickly pear cactus and drew back sharply.
Recovering himself, he stopped and studied the spike-
covered plant, whose joints were formed like thick
green paddles. Some even called them paddle cactus
or beavertail cactus because of their shape.

"Say—" Scotty nodded and pursed his lips. "Sure!"

"What's with you?" Danny asked soberly.

"It's been a long time, Danny, since we've roasted
prickly pear cactus over a fire and eaten it. But it
tastes pretty good when you're hungry!"

"Hey!" Danny's smile was in full agreement. "You
are so right! Have you got matches?"

"Always," Scotty replied, "when I'm on the desert.
Dad's always told me to remember that." He glanced

p toward the lowering sky. "Matches are for warmth
—and for light—and for food! That's a desert code!"

"OK, OK, let's just get with it."

With long sticks they separated big top sections of
ie cactus, held them over a fire while they roasted,
nd then peeled back the skin with any lingering
»rickles. The cactus tasted like okra without salt,
»ut it did satisfy their hunger and took care of their
ieed.

"Where to from here?" Scotty asked.

Danny picked up one of his feet and massaged it
enderly. The first clap of thunder sounded in the
listance. They were in a land of rock ledges, scattered
nesquite trees and cactus and great boulders. It was
t sudden, very faint voice that answered Scotty's
juestion.

"Where am I? *Oh, where am I?*" A cry of agony.
A boy's cry who was in torment.

Scotty sucked in his breath. Automatically one
iand reached out to grip Danny's wrist. "You hear
hat?"

"No fooling!"

"Somewhere just in front of us." Scotty took a
itep forward on his sore toes. "Take it slow-like,
Danny."

They walked as though they were treading on rot-
en eggs. Scotty went around the rocks on one side,
Danny on the other. What they saw was the boy Pete,
just a little older than themselves, writhing near a
greasewood bush.

Scotty crept to Pete's side slowly, ready for anything. Danny did the same. They met together, wide-
eyed and afraid.

"What'll we do?" Danny was looking to his friend for the answer, but Scotty just looked back at Danny.

"I guess we'd better pray for him. I've never seen anything like this. I don't know what to do."

*   *   *

When Pete had seemed to fail in his effort to get back into his body, he finally fell unconscious beside it.

Time passed. His eyelids flickered, closed again. He was deep, so deep. More peaceful now. If he could just go on deeper and deeper, perhaps he would never have to come back and face the stark reality of this world again.

Hands pressed him back gently. Cool fingers touched his forehead. From the pressure on his forehead he knew that someone was near. He was back in his body then. Pete felt terribly grateful for that.

Sand and dirt were caked in his shoulder-length hair, and his poncho was wadded beneath his limp body.

His bare feet were covered with cuts from which blood oozed slowly.

Jesus. Pete tossed restlessly. He was coming in for a rough landing. He didn't know anything about Jesus, had never heard His name except in cursing. But he knew God. He *did* know God. And—God had let him down.

Pete's lips opened, and he mumbled something the fellows could not understand. Very slowly his words became more distinct and, as the sounds took new form, new panic and near frenzy took hold of him.

"You didn't come today, God." His voice rose until it became an angry shout. "Why didn't You come to

me when I needed You? Where were You, God?" As
he continued to ramble, the loudness left his voice.
With a shudder he sank back, exhausted, turned onto his stomach, buried his face in his dirty arms and
sobbed like a lonely, broken child. "I need You, God,
and You haven't come to me. Where are You, God?
Oh, where—where have You gone?"

The hands that had touched him a moment ago
became arms, strong and gentle, that cradled his head.
Pete turned his head to look into the face of the one
who was kneeling beside him. The wildness was really
beginning to fade away, and he was becoming more
rational. The nightmare was falling into the background, and he was coming through whole.

Whole. Lying there in a boy's arms, Pete reached
down and felt for his legs. Yes, he was whole again.
And Pete gave a last mighty sob and tried to sit up.

At last there was quiet. Scotty laid Pete's head
back on the ground, but he continued to sit beside
him. One hand lingered on Pete's arm. Danny was
sitting on his haunches a few feet away, and he was
praying.

Pete offered no resistance. His shaggy head never
moved. Once he spoke. "Please—talk to me. Help
me. Say anything, just talk."

Scotty looked at Danny helplessly. What could
they say? The very atmosphere was charged with
gloom and despair. In desperation Scotty began to
speak, his lips forming the only words that could ever
help—really help—Pete and bring peace to his
troubled heart.

" 'For God so loved the world—' " He hesitated
and started again. " 'For God so loved *Pete* that he

gave his only begotten Son, that who—that if Pete—
believeth in him, he should not perish but have everlasting life.'" Scotty continued gently: "'That they
might know thee, the only true God, and Jesus Christ
whom thou hast sent.'"

Pete closed his eyes. The only true God—Jesus
Christ whom He sent—Strange words coming from
a youth who was at least two years younger than he.
"Scotty? When'd you find me?"

"About thirty or forty minutes ago. I don't know
for sure. We almost gave up finding you. I'm glad
we didn't."

Pete sniffed. "I guess I'm glad."

"Freak out?"

Pete nodded a couple of times. "Freaked out. I
lost consciousness of my body. I wanted to die, the
fear was so horrible. The things I saw, the way I
felt. Like—like I was someone else. And I went
places. Seemed like my spirit had left my body behind and I walked through all kinds of places. There
were snakes and all kinds of horrible creatures following me, touching me." He shuddered and lay back
again. "They were real. Say whatever you want, I
know they were real. I was walking outside of my
body and I know!"

Danny's nostrils flared and his whole face twisted.
How awful! *Ugh!* The very thought of the picture
Pete was painting for them made him have the creeps
like he'd never had creeps! And all because Pete
thought he'd found God through LSD. Wonder what
Pete did contact out there that made him think it
was God?

Scotty's whole body was drawn up tight and his

eyes were a piercing brown. "And—your god didn't come, did he?"

Pete's gaze was clearing now and it flashed to the younger boy's face. "God—" he said sadly. "He didn't come."

"We'd better try to find shelter or something," Scotty said. "You'll never make it down the mountain this evening."

Pete's strange copper eyes were still on Scotty. "Say what you were going to say."

Scotty clamped his teeth hard and his jawbone jutted out a little. "OK, Pete. But listen to me carefully. God never has given anyone His presence through lysergic acid—or any other drug—because you can't put Him in a test tube and make a pill out of Him. You—you have to find Him through Jesus, Pete. I don't know any other way to say it."

Protest was in Pete's voice. "But He used to come to me, always! I know He did! In California, when I first joined the hippies, I found Him in the white-caps, on the beach, in the trees, the park. I found Him everywhere! And He was real, Scotty, He was real!" Pete was about to sob again. His nerves and emotions had been beaten and lashed; and now it was impossible to control them.

Scotty swallowed. Oh, he didn't want to say it wrong! He didn't want to hurt Pete. "Didn't—you remember, Dad asked you! Didn't this presence you felt ever tell you about Jesus? How He died on the cross for you, gave His own blood so you could really know Him?"

Pete shook his head and little particles of dirt flaked off his long hair. "No." *That they may know*

*thee, the only true God, and Jesus Christ whom thou
hast sent.*

The sky had continued to darken with the threaten-
ing storm, and now the sun burst from the clouds
long enough to dip over the horizon. When it did,
Danny spotted a cave just across the little ravine by
which they sat.

"Hey, Scot, look over there! What a perfect place
to spend the night! *If,*" he emphasized, "there aren't
any wild animals there ahead of us!"

"You're right, Danny." Scotty's father's handgun,
which all this time had dangled somewhat awkwardly
at his side, now reminded him of something. He drew
the .32 revolver and aimed it at the sky. "So Dad
and Mother will know we're all OK. Remember,
Danny?"

Scotty shot three times into the air, checked the
gun and replaced it in the holster at his side. Then,
helping Pete who was nervous and brooding, they
headed for the narrow ravine, a gash in the earth
that was deep but narrow enough to leap easily. And
the last ray of sunlight fell into the mouth of the
cave like the beckoning hand of refuge and safety.

"Think we can get Pete across that ravine?"

"Sure," Danny answered. And with his words the
first big spattering drops of rain began to fall. The
sunshine disappeared and clouds began to rise from
all around the horizon.

The fellows kept Pete on his feet and guided him
toward the cave. Danny stepped across first and saw
that the ravine had ripped the earth apart for thirty
feet straight down. Holding out a hand to Pete, the
boys pushed and pulled until he was safely across

the ravine. Pete was still very nervous, and the drops of rain falling on his face seemed to torment him as much as a mass of buzzing flies.

Once they were on the other side of the narrow gorge, they hesitated. From a long distance, there was the sound of rifle shots. Three of them. Scotty smiled with relief.

"Sure took him a long time!" Danny cried softly.

Scotty nodded. It had taken his father a few minutes to answer the shots, but they sounded awfully good. Muffled yet reverberating through the canyons. The boys knew that all was well below.

Two jackrabbits darted by, their ears laid back, sprinting toward their burrows. A lonely bobcat slipped easily along the game trail and out of sight, whether chasing the rabbits, the fellows could not determine.

Scotty, half supporting Pete, pointed just above them. "The cave is right there. Shall we find out if we're going to have it to ourselves or if we'll have to share it with an animal?"

Danny gave his friend a lopsided grin. "Let's just find that out!"

They helped Pete up the slope. Reaching it, they were surprised to find a wide ledge running outside the mouth of the cave. Scotty and Danny looked at each other, and then Scotty motioned with his hand. They peered inside.

"Well, it seems to be all right." There was a little tremor in Danny's voice. "Shall we go inside and get out of the rain?"

Thunder pealed through the heavens. The sky was growing darker continually. Scotty took one back-

ward look before entering the cave. What caught his
attention was a grave marker on the rocky slope.
But they were inside the cave before it struck him.
A grave marker. A grave!

*Find the grave of Jacob Wisner and you have
found the Lost Dutchman Mine!*

12

THE FACE OF AN APACHE

"OH NO!" Scotty moaned softly.

"What's the matter?" Danny asked. Already he was helping Pete to a sitting position and was getting ready to sit down beside him. "Are you getting wet, Scot?"

"It's not that." Scotty thrust his head out into the blinding rain and looked again. "Wait for me!" he cried. "I'll be right back."

"Where—"

But Scotty had already rushed out the cave's opening and slipped and slid his way to the old grave marker. He was drenched, but it didn't seem to matter. Hunching down close and shielding his eyes from the pelting rain, he scanned the marker for a name. There it was, crudely scrawled.

J-a-c-o-b W-i-s-n-e-r. Jacob Wisner!

Scotty looked up slowly toward the gray outline of the cave's mouth. They had stumbled onto the Lost Dutchman Mine!

What new dangers awaited them here? If the stories and legends were true, and there were really Apache sentries who guarded this gold, what would keep the Indians from stumbling onto the boys sooner or later? After all, the guards were fully aware of the camping

party, or the rockslide would never have occurred.
Nor the wild laughter that was supposed to be that
of the old Dutchman.

"Maybe we ought to get out of here now and head
for— But we can't!" Scotty cried, answering himself
before the sentence was formed. "Pete can't make it!"

He hesitated, looking all around before dashing
back to the mine opening. Now that he knew where
he was, there was an uncanny fear that wanted to
dog him.

Breathing hard, Scotty sat down by Pete and
Danny. He was cold and uncomfortable, and his
dark hair lay in wet strands over his forehead. He
leaned close to Danny.

"What's the matter?" Danny's eyes looked very
large in the semidarkness.

"We're in the Lost Dutchman Mine!" Scotty
breathed soberly.

"The mine!"

"Shhh!"

"Looks like any ordinary cave to me!" Danny
insisted.

Pete's shaggy head twisted to his far right. He was
trembling and nervous, but he was sane. "It's not!" he
hissed. "Not if there's a tunnel behind this rock!"

Scotty turned his body until he could see behind the
rock where they were sitting. There was a dark,
yawning hole there, all right. It even looked inviting
—a refuge from this shallow cave where they sat
trying to keep away from the blowing rain.

The heavens belched forth thunder that echoed
through the hills, and lightning split in two a pine
tree across the ravine. Yellow flames licked up and

down the stately tree, and finally it careened toward the earth in two parts. The air was gray with spilling rain, and the wind seemed to catch it by the bucketful and dash it at them there in the cave.

Drenched and shivering—not to mention the hunger that was gnawing at them—they drew back as far as possible to keep out of the rain. But it was no use.

"Did I say something about a tunnel?" Pete asked suddenly, his thin body quaking from both cold and fear.

"Yeah. Why?"

"I didn't really think about it when I said it. Now it's starting to hit me. I think I've been here before. Can't—" He put his head in his hands and rubbed at his dirty face. "Can't seem to remember too much. There—there was a room, I think. Big room. And it was warm and dry." He gritted his teeth. "There was something about that room, man, but—I can't remember what it was."

"Well, did you see any Apache Indians? Did there seem to be any danger in the room?"

Pete thought about it. "I didn't see anyone." A chill seized his body. "I just remember that it w-was warm a-and dry and g-good." Suddenly the old untamed look was back in his eyes. He gazed first at Danny and then, lingeringly, at Scotty. "Who—are you?" In a crouch, he rose and backed away from the fellows, until he was standing with his back in the rain. Water dripped from his long hair and from his chin and fingertips. "What am I d-doing here?" He threw both hands across his face. "Who—who am I?"

Scotty felt a strange kind of fear mingle with the

compassion he felt for Pete. What a hideous thing
LSD!

"I thought he was all right," Danny murmured.

Scotty swallowed. "So did I."

"Who am I?" Pete rubbed his eyes. "Please tel
me who I am."

Scotty went to him and pulled him back inside the
wet cave. "Your name is Pete and you're OK. Come
on, Pete, come with us."

They had to get Pete out of this weather. Why, he
had had no food all day. He'd suffered the worst kind
of "freak out" on the acid. And now, if he caught
cold in this storm, anything could happen. Scotty
and his friend could only pray that God would keep
Pete's mind and bring back his memory.

Passively Pete followed the boys down the twisting
tunnel. The Apaches were certainly keeping the place
in good condition. The walls of the tunnel had been
bricked in to prevent falling dirt and strengthen it
against a possible cave-in. The floor was even and
hard-packed. But it was dark and lonely in the tunnel.
Creepy.

It did not last long, however. The tunnel was short
and came to an abrupt ending as it emerged into a
great rock chamber that was lighted by some unseen
opening from above.

Scotty started and he felt Danny grab his arm. The
scene that was before them was nearly unbelievable.
Looms of all sizes sat in the chamber—weaving looms
upon which were half-finished rugs, blankets, ponchos
Ponchos! Scotty looked quickly from the pile of finished ponchos nearby to the one Pete was wearing.
Identical!

It seemed impossible! Pete had stolen his poncho from this very room! He *had* been here before, indeed. And no one had seen or caught *or* killed him! Well, then! Surely the three of them could rest here just until the storm was over! But where could this famed ledge of pure gold be? Scotty's heart started beating faster at the thought. So close. Never thought he'd be that close to the Lost Dutchman Mine! And brought into it, practically, by a hippie.

Evidently Danny was feeling the same way. His blue eyes darted here and there, and they were shining with hopeful dreams.

"Who am I?" Pete muttered slowly.

"It's all right, Pete," Scotty assured him. "You'll be all right."

Upon a closer look, the two boys saw the various dyes used in the Apache designs, the strange spools of wool, all hand-spun. On the other side of the room were supple handsewn boots and moccasins. There were hundreds of rawhide laces and various pieces and sizes of soft leather with which to work.

Scotty stroked back his hair, dried now into crisp, heavy strands. A frown marked his freckled forehead. A little smile played about his lips.

"What a temptation!" he whispered to Danny.

They looked down at their bruised, cut feet. How easy to just take a pair of those soft moccasins. Why, they could even leave their billfolds and whatever money was in them. But their hearts told them this was not the way.

"Who am I?" Pete whispered in agony.

The hippie had wandered over to a massive pile of finished rugs and had lain down. His countenance was anguished, and his eyes were wild, haunted. The boys rushed to him and knelt at his side, trying to assure him that he was going to be all right, that this was not going to last.

Scotty looked at Pete and saw his classmate Dave. Dave, who would never be right again. Dave, who would spend his years in a state mental institution because of this same drug. Dave, pounding the cells with bloody fists and crying through the night hours, "Who am I? Who am I? Won't someone please tell me who I am?"

Scotty moved away from Pete and went to stand by himself in the shadows of the room. He prayed softly, "Pete was looking for You, God. Surely, surely You'll see to it that he finds You—the right way! The devil had him so fooled. Show him that You're real and that Jesus loves him."

"Where am I?" Pete cried.

They tried to hush him. It would be too dangerous if he became loud and violent there.

The three of them rested on the soft, warm rugs. After some time Pete fell into a fitful sleep. Danny drowsed from time to time. The darkness inside the chamber became as black as carbon. It was night. Scotty was awake for some time, arms folded beneath his head, heart beating fast—hoping, praying that his folks were safe. And then he too slept.

Scotty never knew when he awakened; but he would never forget the light shining into his face and the bronzed face that peered down at him. A big face with anger flashing in the black eyes. A face with the emblem of a cross branded upon his forehead!

13

GOLD OF THE THUNDER-GODS

FOR WHAT SEEMED a breathless lifetime, Scotty stared into the angry black eyes. His mind had gone numb and he couldn't think. He hardly breathed.

The light played over Danny and Pete, and the Apache sucked in his breath at sight of the poncho Pete was wearing. In the half light Scotty saw the bewilderment in the Indian's eyes. Otherwise his face was that of any stoic Indian.

In one swift movement the Apache's arm reached out and jerked Scotty to his feet. The rough sound of the Indian's voice brought both Danny and Pete to full wakefulness.

Danny got to his hands and knees. "Hey! What's going on? Hey!"

Pete too was awake and seemed more alert. He looked much like an Apache himself at the moment. Long, wild hair, dark eyes, swarthy skin, poncho. Even the Apache gave him a third look.

The Indian towered above them. By the light of his lantern he surveyed the boys with hate and anger, then he spit on the ground at their feet.

"Mister, we just want to get down off this mountain! We didn't come here on purpose. It was storming and we wanted to get in out of the rain." Scotty spread his hands helplessly. "Honest, if you'll just help us find our way back down the mountain, we'll sure appreciate it."

The black eyes grew cunning. He burst forth with such a flow of language that it left the boys startled. A moment later a woman entered the big room, a woman who cowered back of her husband and waited. He shouted something to her without looking around, and then he yanked Pete to his feet and shoved all three of them toward the far side of the room.

The Apache woman followed in silence, her many flowing skirts rustling about her ankles.

"Why does the white man not learn that he is invading a sacred mountain by coming here? This belongs to the Apache alone!" The black eyes narrowed. "Every white man, woman or boy who comes to look for the Apache's gold will be stalked by misfortune."

They went down a short, narrow passage that was filled with the smell of dirty sweatbands that the Apaches wore about their foreheads, of dirt and of strange food.

Presently they came into another large room. In the dim light of the swaying lantern, the boys saw several adults sleeping on thick woolen blankets which had been woven on the looms in the other room. Here was where the odor of cooking had risen. Beans, fried bread and mutton. The smell of stale coffee hung in the air.

What a setup! Scotty thought. *The guards must change every now and then. They bring their wives along and just keep right on with their weaving and making things as if they were on the reservation. Wow!*

There was a kind of alcove at the end of this room. The Apache pushed and shoved the boys toward it without hesitating. As the light filled the space before them, there appeared to be a great ledge of yellowish gold. It was endless in the eerie light and surely represented a vast fortune. A vein of purest gold. They were standing before the shrine of the Apaches—their sacred shrine, raw gold—placed there, they believed, by the thunder-gods for their use in time of need. No wonder they could take amounts of this gold to the mint and return mysteriously with herds, flocks, horses and other things that were necessary to their way of life.

The ledge of gold, so famed throughout the States, would have held Scotty and Danny spellbound indefinitely, except for the rough hands that pushed them forward. Scotty was beginning to wonder if the whole mountain was hollow!

With steps that made no sound at all, the Apache turned the boys suddenly into a small room. Apparently the storm had ended a long time ago, for rays of pale moonlight filtered into the room. Where they came from, however, was a mystery.

The Apache set down his lantern, spoke for a moment to the Indian woman, then turned his attention to the fellows. The cross on his forehead looked more like a tattoo now that Scotty was fully awake, and it left a great question mark in the boy's mind.

Evidently the Apache loathed to speak English, for, though he looked at the boys long and hard, he uttered not a word. With a mighty shove, he sent them flying across the room and onto a pile of filthy, tattered blankets. Other than these blankets, there was nothing in the room but a crude table and three high-powered rifles standing in a corner. Someone must use this room for sleeping, for it had the same smell of sweat and fried bread.

The Indian woman was left to take up guard at the door, and there she made herself comfortable on the rough floor, a rifle cradled across her folded arms. Her face was like bronzed stone, her eyes like Apache Tears.[1] There was a strange kind of peace about her face.

The lantern was gone, and there were only the faint moonbeams left to filter through. What would the morning bring? Scotty thrust out his lower lip. Would it bring—death? For who had ever come near this place and lived? Much less one who actually stumbled into the cave! Would it mean death to Pete also? Pete—poor, lonely Pete.

"What are ya doin'?"

Scotty lifted his head. "I'm not sure. Thinking. Or praying. Maybe both."

"What do you figure's going to happen to us, Scot?" Danny asked.

Scotty tried hard to chuckle. "Well, I hope we'll all get out of here all right!"

Pete lifted his sad eyes. "I don't want to live," he whispered hoarsely.

"Oh, sure you do!" Danny protested.

"I want to die." And with that, the miserable piece of filth and flesh seemed to crumble.

Scotty forgot their predicament. Flinging himself

---

[1] A black stone searched for and rubbed to smoothness, then treasured as a good-luck piece by its Indian owner.

at Pete's feet, he cried, "Pete, don't say that! You have to live! You have to live to know God—to know Jesus!"

"I thought I knew God," Pete said quietly.

Scotty's eyes pleaded with Pete. "It was Satan!" When Scotty said the words, they suddenly burst upon him like a ray of sunlight. Sure! Sure, that's who it was! "Listen, Pete. The Bible says that Satan can be transformed into an angel of light. When you're on a trip with LSD, you can meet the devil and think it's God, because he comes to you and tries to pass himself off as God. That's what he did away back there thousands of years ago. He decided that he was going to be God, and he was thrown out of heaven. But he never stopped trying. He tried it with you; he tried to make you think he was God."

Pete's eyes narrowed. He was trying desperately to understand. "But—if what you're telling me is true— he *did* fool me. I *did* believe it. Why?"

Scotty lowered his eyes and then lifted them quickly. He put out an earnest hand. "Because you never knew the presence of God before! How could you have been sure? Pete, listen now. It's just like Dad told you. If it had been God, He would have drawn you to His Son Jesus. You can go to heaven only if you know Jesus. But—you can never find Him on LSD. You have to come to Jesus Christ like me and everyone else and take Him as your Saviour. You have to confess your sins and ask Him to wash them away with His blood. Then, when you know Him, you'll find out you know God too. And He will walk with you every moment without the acid, and you'll know His presence."

Pete's gaze never left Scotty's face. No one had told him these things before. No one ever cared enough. But Pete felt faith in his heart and he knew that all Scotty said was true.

"How—how can I know Him?"

"Talk to Him—ask Him to come into your life, to save you. He'll come the minute you ask."

Pete waited no longer. It didn't matter that the other guys were there. Nor the Apache woman. Pete opened his mouth and started talking to God and the first thing they knew, he was bawling. It was OK. He'd needed it for so long.

Maria, the Indian woman, thrust her head around the corner. Amazement was upon her heavy features. She made a move as though to come into the room, but seconds later she changed her mind and took up her position again.

For a moment Scotty pondered the cross upon the Apache's forehead and breathed in the aroma of fresh coffee. Somehow it overtook the smell of unclean bodies and perspiration.

Pete knew Christ, and it showed all over him. His shoulders had a set of dignity to them, of determination. His eyes were clear. He was still taken up with the unmistakable presence of the true God and of Jesus Christ, His Son!

It grew somewhat lighter inside their prison. A kind of gray light. Scotty wondered why their captor had allowed them to view the ledge of pure gold even for a moment. Of course he probably meant to kill them anyway. Even if he didn't—which would be a miracle—the boys could never find their way down the mountain now. Scotty doubted seriously that they could even find their way from under this mountain very soon.

Bronzed hands appeared, stretching toward Maria, who took something from them. A moment later she lifted her heavy body and the multitude of skirts from the floor and labored toward them. In her hands was a tray woven of straw, and upon it were cracked cups holding coffee, bits of corn and mutton and several pieces of fried bread. After so long a time, without food, anything looked good.

Danny reached out as though to touch the woman's hand. "Ma'am? What—what are you going to do with us?"

Scotty watched the woman closely. Her black eyes moved over each boy there. Suddenly Scotty saw her, not as an Apache Indian, but as a woman who knew pain and fear and love, just as his own mother knew them. Why, this Indian, though wrinkled and bent, was probably no older than his own mother. It made him feel sad for her to have to live such a life.

The woman did not reply. Pete was watching her, waiting for an answer.

"Will they—*kill* us?" Scotty dared to ask.

The woman's eyes turned to the freckle-faced youth and lingered there. "I don't know," she replied slowly.

Scotty swallowed. "Ma'am? Is it all right if I call you Maria?" Scotty thought he detected a faint smile, but if there was one, it was quickly masked. The woman gave a slow incline of her head. "Maria," Scotty went on, "why did the man—the one who found us—have the mark of the cross on his forehead?"

The woman folded her arms proudly. "He is one of the original Apaches."

"What do you mean?" All three boys were sitting forward with interest now.

"Don't you know that the Apache is the outcast, the outlaw? They are Indians who were put from their own tribes and then came together for their own protection. These outlaws were branded as outlaws by having the mark of a cross tattooed on their foreheads. José is in a straight line from the first Apache."

"I think she means he's a direct descendant," Pete said.

"Won't you help us?" Danny begged.

"We don't care anything about the mine," Scotty said. "We were just trying to find Pete, here; and when we did, it began to storm and we found the cave. That's all."

"We'd never find it again," Danny continued. "We don't even know if we can find Scotty's folks."

"Your parents are on the mountain?" Maria asked.

"They're down below waiting for us." Scotty bit into the fried bread eagerly.

Maria's rather flat face seemed to sink even more. She dropped her gaze and, now that it was daylight, studied the fellows' feet. "How did that happen?" she asked, pointing.

"There was a rockslide at our camp," Scotty explained. "It would have killed every one of us, except that halfway down the mountain it turned and buried our jeep and almost everything else, except what we had on."

"Shoes included," Danny offered.

"We had to find Pete," Scotty said doggedly. "Shoes or no shoes."

Maria had frowned at mention of the rockslide. Almost as if she had known about it but disapproved heartily. She continued to look at the cuts and dried blood on the boys' feet. Then, without any trace of emotion, she turned and passed from the room.

"I feel pretty good as long as that big Apache's not here," Danny said.

"Yeah. But he'll be back. You wait," Pete warned. "Listen! I hear someone coming right now!"

14

THE HALF-BREED

DANNY HAD BEEN SIPPING the strong coffee for lack of anything else to drink. Hearing the heavy steps he placed the stained cup back on the tray.

The fried bread lost its flavor in Scotty's mouth and he braced himself for whatever was coming.

Pete's face did not change, nor did he show by the flicker of an eyelash that he was troubled. Perhaps it was because he had been through so much on his last and final trip on LSD that nothing could shake him now.

The three of them waited quietly. Breathlessly they listened as Maria spoke with someone. Was it the Apache who had discovered them inside the cave? Their wonder turned to complete bewilderment when a man stepped into the little rock room—a man with white skin and blue eyes.

None of the boys moved. Their expressions changed, but they neither spoke nor moved.

The stranger stood looking them over, then he leaned back against the cold wall and propped a booted foot on the table.

The coffee swished uncertainly in the cups and a little went over the side of Danny's cup. He didn't care. He hated coffee anyway, but it had been something to drink.

Maria came softly into the room, but, as any Indian woman would do, she made no offer to introduce the man. Rather, she kept her place in the background and simply watched the proceedings.

"Fellows," the man said at last, "you can relax. Nothing is going to hurt you. Matter of fact—" He paused, dug into his watch pocket for a toothpick and stuck it in the corner of his mouth. "I'm really here to help you." He gestured toward the Apache woman. "I'm Maria's half brother."

"No fooling!" Scotty burst out without meaning to. "Why, you look just like any other—That is—"

Maria did not smile, but the man grinned as if it didn't bother him in the least. "We had different mothers," he explained, "and mine was a white woman."

A half-breed, Scotty thought. Boy, what a twist!

"And you can come and go as you please?" Danny asked, awed.

"That's right. I'm their half brother. I live at the foot of the Superstitions, and I can wander about as I want to. They can trust me and they know it."

Scotty moistened his lips. "What—I mean, why—why are you here now?"

"Maybe I happened up here because three boys and a family below need my help." He raised his bushy black brows. "The help, I might add, that only I can give them."

"What do you mean?" Pete asked.

"Well in the first place, José would kill you tonight

if Maria had not gotten word to me and asked me to help you down the mountain."

Danny swallowed hard and his eyes almost popped.

The intense look in Pete's eyes screamed a single word. *No!* Pete had just found life, and he wanted to spend it with his hair cut and some clean clothes and a bath.

"Where do you fit in?" Scotty asked. He really wanted to cross the room and throw his arms around Maria, but he only gave her a look of gratitude.

"I'm leaving here in ten minutes. I met your parents this morning, but of course none of us were sure where you were at that time. I took them to a place where they could spend the night in safety, and they're waiting for me to bring you down." He studied the boys' feet and spoke to Maria, who disappeared immediately on some bidden chore.

"By the way," the man said, "my name is John, and you can trust me to the full."

"We sure do thank you, John," Scotty said with feeling. "If we could ever have made it back to the little cave that led us here, maybe—just maybe—we could have found our way back. And I can see why José would want to get us out of the way. We saw the gold!"

John smiled knowingly. "You saw but a speck of the gold on your way here. The actual shrine of virgin gold has never been seen by any outsider except the old Dutchman. No white man shall see the shrine and live!"

The faces of the boys fell. But at least they *had* seen more gold than they ever dreamed possible. That was something.

"As for your finding your way back down the
mountain from that small opening into this mine,
never! You see, the storm caused a mud and rock
slide during the night and it filled the cave so completely that the Apaches will probably leave it that
way."

"But that was the way into the cave!" Danny protested.

"It was *one* way," John corrected. "If you had gone
to sleep there, you would have been sealed in and
drowned. It's impossible to tell that the opening was
over there. That's why Maria and I feel it's safe to
lead you away from here. You have no story to tell,
really."

Scotty cocked his head. *Well, I don't know,* he
thought. *It still seems exciting to me.*

At that moment Maria appeared again, this time
holding several pairs of soft moccasin-type boots in
her hands. John took them from her and passed three
pairs to the boys. With looks of thankfulness, the fellows slipped them on. They were slightly large, but
they would see them down the Superstitions.

John left the room, only to return with his canteen
filled with water. He offered a drink to the boys, which
they accepted eagerly. Before leaving the room, Scotty
took up a piece of fried bread to eat on the way. He
stopped beside Maria and awkwardly took her plump
hand.

"Thank you, Maria. Thanks a lot!"

She looked at him strangely. Just the barest trace
of a smile touched her face, and then again she was
the stoic Apache who showed no emotion.

John led the boys blindfolded down a maze of

tunnels. Bright sunlight burst upon them at last, bu
the blindfolds were not removed for a half hour. The
led one another by holding hands. John led them s
carefully and knew his way so well that not once di
the fellows slip or fall.

When their eyes were free finally, the country wa
completely new to them. They went downward now
and once John cautioned them to stop and crouc
behind some brush. John had the eyes and ears of th
Apache. Apparently they were a little too near to on
of the sentries. When John walked, it was with silen
feet, and never did he speak aloud on that downwar
trip.

It was one-thirty when Scotty began to recogniz
the land, but it was in another, smaller valley tha
they came upon the Hanson family.

There were cries of thankfulness and relief. Ever
Susan looked good. Everyone was talking at once fo
a time and Pete hung back, unable to enter into
family situation.

It was Mrs. Hanson who went to Pete, looked int
his eyes for a moment, then laid her warm hand along
side his face. "Pete, are you all right?"

Pete didn't draw away. He stood and looked a
her and his lower lip quivered. "Please, ma'am.
don't want to burst out bawling again."

She took her hand away and a feeling of eas
came between them. "When did that happen?" sh
asked, smiling.

"Last night."

She cocked her head and her blue eyes penetrate
his copper ones. "Last night?"

"Yes, Mrs. Hanson. I—" Pete looked down at his moccasins. "I found God last night."

"Oh, Pete!"

"No, ma'am," Pete said hurriedly, "not—not on LSD." No need to explain his freak-out. She wouldn't understand that. "I mean I found the real God—the God in the Bible. I asked Jesus Christ to forgive my sins."

"Pete, I'm so thrilled! We were all praying. We knew that Scotty and Danny were with you or they would have returned. I'm so glad!" she said again.

Pete lifted his eyes and there was a new assurance there. "I bragged about how God would take care of me and help me get you off the mountain. It didn't work that way at all. Then I saw how the real God took care of Scotty and Danny and—" He looked at the woman wistfully. "I wanted *Him*."

Scotty was listening in and his heart gave a leap at Pete's testimony. Oh, that he could tell everyone in the world that one cannot find God through LSD.

15

THE RETURN TRIP

JOHN BROUGHT CHOCOLATE BARS, raisins and crackers from the pockets of his soft leather jacket. Then drinking long from a mountain spring, the group began the long trek down the mountain.

John wore a wide-brimmed hat, and beneath that hat it was easy to see that he had the color and flatness of nose that were typical of the Apache. Only his blue eyes, his speech and his openness to others said that he was a half-breed.

The Indian chose paths that were hidden to the eyes of the white man. It was an easy way, where no one had ever disturbed the wild life of these parts. Cottontails, deer, quail and even javelina pigs were to be seen in abundance.

"Some vacation!" Scotty grinned. He surveyed the rest of the group. Crumpled clothing, weary faces, everyone's hair disheveled—creeping along a clean-cut path that was completely hidden by brush and overhanging mesquite limbs. "What a straggly bunch!"

"You don't look very good either," Danny groaned. "Your clothes are a mess. And you're so scratched up I'd hardly take you for a human being!" He clucked his tongue. "I don't think I'd want to be seen with you on the street."

Pete took this lightness joyfully. "Be thankful you don't look like a girl wearing a dirty, stolen poncho."

They laughed together. What a nightmare had been left in the Superstition Mountains. Yes, they'd been through a lot together.

"I feel good about you, Pete," Danny said soberly.

"What're you going to do when you get back to Phoenix?" This had been a matter of real concern with Scotty.

Pete immediately grew serious. "What would you do?" he said, giving the question right back to Scotty. Then, before the dark-haired youth could reply, Pete continued. "My mom's a drunk. She's a sot! She never saw a person in the whole world but herself." His eyes narrowed. "My dad's not so bad—swears a lot. Tells me to get out of the house. But, considering my mom, I guess he's OK."

"Then—" Scotty swallowed painfully. "You really don't have a home to go back to?"

Pete shook his head. "No, I don't. And I want to be around straight people. I know I can't go back to the hippies." He ducked to prevent the thorns of a cactus from pricking his shoulder. "So—what would you do?"

"I'd go to the Youth Center," Danny broke in simply.

Pete squinted. "Youth Center? What's that?"

Scotty smiled. "Just what the name says. It's a big home, really, there in Phoenix. I've never seen it, but I've heard a lot about it. And this couple who run it take in guys like you who've messed around with drugs. They take care of you, give you a bed and food. And they try to lead these fellows to Jesus. They can stay as long as they want to. You see, Pete, there's more than coming to Christ. You need His strength to live for Him in the world. This all comes through prayer and studying the Bible. That's the whole reason for this center."

Pete's eyes bugged. "They do all this for you—*free*? Look, if this fairy tale is true, somebody's got to pay for it."

"Somebody does. A whole lot of somebodys. They send money, bring food and furniture. I'd sure like to see you go there, Pete."

He looked at himself. "Would they want *me?*"

"They'd be so glad if you'd come."

Pete remembered the tender hand of Mrs. Hanson touching his face. It would be terrific to live in a place where there was love. "I think," he said dreamily, "that's where I'll go. I fooled around so long. But I *have* found God!"

Scotty blocked the path for a moment to stare at Pete. "I don't think you found Him," he declared. "I think God saw you blundering around all over the Superstitions, and He couldn't stand to see you suffer any longer—so He came and found *you.*"

Pete thought it over and a grin broke over his face. "I think you're right, Scot!"

John had broken into a small clearing and headed for a Ford Bronco which was camouflaged by brush. "Climb aboard," he shouted, "and I will have you all back in Phoenix in about three hours."

A general sigh of relief and gladness went up as the party got into the Bronco. And just in time; for the sun had already dipped over the horizon and a chill had fallen over the mountains. Another adventure had dropped its curtain and they must all head back for home and all the things that home meant.